THE RUSTED BLADE

NICHOLAS KOTAR

WAYSTONE
PRESS

CHAPTER 1

THE WARRIOR'S PENTAGON

Dust on the air rose in cloudlets from the sandy ground. It was fine, slightly sweet on Otchigen's tongue. The silence stretched, tense with the expectation of cheering. A single drop of sweat labored down Otchigen's craggy forehead. Forcing his hand not to brush it away—a warrior does not pay attention to such things—he crouched to the sand. Caressing it, he let it run through his fingers, gentler even than the soft touch of his wife. He closed his eyes and drank it all in. Ecstasy bloomed inside him.

Today was the final mock battle in the warriors' seminary of Vasyllia.

Otchigen, chief warrior of Vasyllia, Mother of Cities, stood up in the middle of the fighters' pentagon, letting the sight of it sink into his bones. The amphitheater seats of carved marble surrounding the pentagon were empty, still half-dark in morning shadow. In the distance rose the three striped and four star-embossed domes crowning the seven towers of the palace. They sparkled like burnished red gold in the summer sun.

It was the sparkle that caused his eyes to water. Yes, it was definitely the sparkle.

Further still, towering over all, the twin falls of Vasyllia plunged down either side of Vasyllia Mountain's summit, where the summer snow glistened, too intense to look at for long. Against the faint hum of the waterfalls, a single birdcall broke into the tedium of repeated sound. As though waiting for it, a choir of birds joined in, and the rest of the silence shattered around Otchigen. At that exact moment, the sun rose over the tip of the amphitheater, warming the back of Otchigen's head.

He laughed at the absurd perfection of it. This was a morning fitting for a demonstration of his young warriors' prowess.

Otchigen turned toward the sun and the deliberately missing fourth wall of the fighting pit. To fighter and viewer alike, that gap in the wall revealed all Vasyllia's three reaches extending down and outward from the heights to the long plateau before the city, cleaved by the Vasyllia River. To call it a city was to ignore the brilliance of it. The mountain itself—crags, groves, waterfall—had been molded into the service of man. Stone cliffs had been made into windowed halls. Arched bridges were carved to span canals, fed from the waters of the twin falls. Groves of wild pine had been tamed into parks and terraces, and now cherries and peaches grew between kitchen gardens set apart from each other by cobbled streets.

Let all the other cities bow in awe and wonder before the Mother of Cities, he thought.

To his left, the iron-barred central gate to the pentagon creaked open. The sandy dust blew outward, as though the seminary were a living thing breathing its warriors out into the world. Karakul walked out of the seminary and into the pit. Otchigen smiled ruefully and shook his head.

Or perhaps not. He might be champion this year. A Karilan. And a foundling to boot.

Karakul hesitated only a moment when he saw that the pentagon wasn't empty, but his angled features relaxed with the cheerful recognition that so flew in the face of the decorum of third-reach Vasyllia.

"My lord Otchigen! You are awake early."

"As are you, Karakul. But that doesn't surprise me."

Karakul blushed. It occurred to Otchigen that if a fair-skinned Vasylli's flush was like a rose suddenly blossoming against snow, then this Karilan reddened like wine poured into a brown clay cup. He had never grown out of seeing their round-bowl faces, flattened noses, and almond eyes as anything but exotic. Certainly not beautiful. But this morning, there was something fascinating about Karakul. He seemed a blood brother to the early sun, the sand underfoot, the hewn marble of the amphitheater and palace. He had their natural joy and strength. And it made him beautiful.

"Well, my mountain eagle," said Otchigen, clapping Karakul on the shoulder. He was pleased to feel the firmness of the muscle under the linen practice shirt. "The amassed greatness of the Vasylli will be cheering against you. It will be like nothing you've ever felt before. Greater men than you have crumbled under it."

Karakul chuckled and shook his head.

"Do you know what my name means in Karilan?" Karakul looked at Otchigen with eyes that caught the sun and shone unexpectedly green. "*Cursed slave*. A name given by my mother."

"I didn't know that," said Otchigen. "A strange gift she gave you. No wonder you wanted to leave Karila."

"No, lord. It was the best gift she could have given." Karakul stared at the falls thoughtfully, as though his mother was some-where beyond Vasyllia Mountain.

There was no sarcasm in his tone. Otchigen, for the first time in as long as he could remember, had no ready response. It unnerved him.

Karakul looked away from the falls and smiled again.

"Oh, don't worry, lord. I'm going to pound that Vasylli lordling into the sand."

Two hours later, the amphitheater seating was packed with restive young warriors—each sitting with his own cohort, in the cohort's colors. The effect was as though some High Being had covered the amphitheater with six heraldic banners—red, cerulean, gold, purple, green, and gold-fringed black. The banners seethed, as though each hid a nest of hornets just waking up to the short, brilliant mountain summer of Vasyllia. Otchigen knew that as soon as the oxhorn blared, the hornets would be up and in a frenzy.

Those same hornets seemed to have woken up in his gut.

To distract himself, he looked at the first cohort in their gold-fringed black. The "Dar's Swords," they called themselves. Surely his son Voran would be there already.

Gold-haired youth after gold-haired youth avoided Otchigen's probing glance. As always, it made Otchigen simmer. He knew he cut an impressive figure with his blacksmith shoulders and the sharp contrast of his wiry black beard, thick as bear hide, with the white braid flowing down his back to his hips. The air of placid domesticity hiding a seething ferocity. It unsettled the boys, as well it should. Rare was the warrior who took it as a challenge, even rarer the man who recognized it as the first step to a warm friendship, reserved for the very few.

Come to think of it, Karakul was the last to acquire his friendship since... he couldn't even remember when.

Voran had never even try to win his father's friendship. He was too remote, too lost in his reveries, his constant inner search for... something.

Why wasn't Voran the one facing Karakul on the mock battle field? That would have been truly fitting.

Then Otchigen remembered. How could he have forgotten? With a twinge of fear tugging at his stomach, Otchigen pushed the thought aside. He had been forgetting things more and more lately.

Voran, Otchigen's only son, had been walled in the far keep of the warrior seminary for two weeks now. The so-called Ordeal of Silence. Otchigen scoffed audibly, he couldn't help himself. The Ordeal of Silence—the storytellers insisted it was the oldest and most difficult of all the warrior ordeals—was rarely practiced any more. Certainly not by 16-year old boys, no matter which reach they hailed from. No noble third-reacher ever allowed his son to attempt it. More often than not it was a second-reacher merchant-son or the rare first-reacher who took the challenge— and then, only because it promised advancement to the third reach. None of them ever made it, of course.

Come to think of it, no one had successfully completed the Ordeal of Silence for at least a hundred years.

And now not only Voran, but the Dar's own son, Prince Mirnían, had decided to brave the silence at the same time.

Otchigen almost wished that Voran had done it to prove himself to his father. Even a defiant call for attention would be welcome. But Otchigen knew that Voran did it for his own reasons, with no thought for Otchigen. Even less thought for Aglaia, his own mother, who would have gladly strewn his road to the ordeal with strawberry blossoms.

Otchigen caught himself actually growling. With an effort, he relaxed the two bunched masses of muscle on either side of his neck. *Flow like water*, he told himself, feeling the strain leech off his body down to the nervously tapping heels of his worn boots.

Mirnían, he knew, did it because he envied Voran. And for what? Did he think mooning about the forests, sleeping under the stars, communing with the winds was the measure of manhood? In Vasyllia? The Mother of Cities? Her warriors were the envy of all fighting men the world over.

The mass of hornets heaved the banners in anticipation.

Otchigen snapped into his war-awareness. The rustle of the distant falls, the creaking of gloved hand on sword-hilt, the wistful moan of a moon-bird—it all washed over him individually and as a symphony of sound. The sharp smell of sweat tickled his nostrils. The rust-fringed door from the seminary halls groaned open. It was time.

Two young warriors walked out side by side. One was resplendent in gilded scale mail over a red shirt, reaching down to the knees of wildly striped breeches of green, gold, and purple. Nevida, the son of Rudin, chief bootlicker of the third reach. Even though he wore his helmet already, the nose guard a gaudy caricature of a horse's muzzle, Otchigen still noted the glint of gold on his ear.

The idiot was already wearing his champion's earring.

Otchigen's smile warmed him to the pit of his stomach. He felt, more than saw, the cohort elders who sat near him shrink unconsciously away from that smile.

Keep the beast within, he chided himself.

Karakul, walking a bit behind Nevida, wore a tail of white horsehair in the peak of his helm. Like all Karilans, he wore no eye guard or nose guard, just a simple conical metal cap. Nor was his armor anything more than simple chain mail over leather and linen. Not a single stripe decorated his stained grey breeches, the same ones he wore to every practice bout. His boots were serviceable. Nothing more.

Then he drew his sword, and all of Nevida's glitz faded as though the sun were covered in a sudden storm cloud. It was an ancient relic of Karila—a double-edged stabbing sword with a metal guard wrought into flowing shapes of waves and tongues of fire so fine, it looked as though it were grown from a tree, not pounded out of crude metal. The edges caught the morning sun and seemed to sing with it.

At the sight of the blade, half of the cohorts hissed. Of the rest, most remained restive, while only a few allowed themselves to cheer. Karakul had done so much to prove himself, and still most Vasylli couldn't forgive him for being an Otherlander.

In a flash of insight, Otchigen realized how much Karakul had trusted him by revealing the meaning of his name. One whiff of the truth, and the entire amphitheater would pelt him with his mother's gift.

Why couldn't you be my son, Karakul?

The guilt only prickled at him as the oxhorns blared. Already, the two combatants were beginning the dance of blades—each choosing a preliminary position based on their relative height, speed, and size. Nevida's stance was an insult in itself—it was a guard against axemen, most of whom were too short to earn the right of bearing a sword.

Karakul was nearly a head taller than Nevida.

For his own part, Karakul took a proper stance—one of humility before a swordmaster. But there was a hint of something about the shape of his sword-arm's sweep... at first, Otchigen couldn't place it.

With a plunge of tingling excitement, Otchigen realized that Karakul was setting Nevida up for a mighty fall.

The fighters danced.

Otchigen, in his war-awareness, missed the sweep and spectacle of the fight—the thing that made the boys in the stands alternately groan and cry out. Like a drunkard who had avoided ale for a week, he thirsted for those nearly invisible details that spoke the true language of the dance—the war dance of hand, foot, elbow, and hip.

Nevida flicked his left hand—a dagger had appeared there as if from nowhere—in a languid attempt at undercutting Karakul's sword arm. Karakul's right knee pushed, relaxed, flexed, then tensed. Otchigen gasped as he saw the move before it even came — a stag-like leap away from Nevida. But he still managed to nick Nevida's left ear with a vicious slash that the Vasylli had never expected. A spray of blood adorned the sand. Karakul leaned back, but the tension in his hip—Otchigen had seen the same anticipation in the body of a Karilan dancer at market day once—proved he was about to leap forward. As Nevida lunged, sure that he had caught Karakul off balance, Karakul spun out of his range of motion, sweeping his blade down as he landed. It sliced down the back side of Nevida's right shoulder.

The Vasylli lordling's blade clattered to the sand, raising a puff of dust.

The fight was over.

The entire city seemed to fall silent.

But something was wrong. No matter what the boys thought about Karakul, the mastery he displayed should outweigh any pettiness. He was their brother after all, even if an Otherlander. Where was the cheering?

Otchigen turned his head around toward the palace.

His heart stopped for a moment. Prince Mirnían stood in the royal box—a turret like an eyrie overlooking the fighters' pentagon. It was carved out of a single block of marble in the shape of an outspreading crown of oak. Like a flower in bloom, the seat of the Dar crowned the top of the tree. Mirnían, with his pale green face and stooping demeanor, looked like a blight on that tree's perfection.

Otchigen silently chided himself for the thought. But the prince looked terrible. His usual grace—the kind that equally attracted the admiration of women and men—was marred. As though a perfectly-shaped peach-colored rose had a single brown petal curling in on itself in the center of the bud, ruining the whole picture.

Metal rang against metal. For a moment, Otchigen was confused, and his head spun as he tried to orient his bulk relative to the new, wrong noise. It was in the pentagon. Nevida had picked up his sword and had attacked Karakul again. Karakul reeled, clearly taken aback.

Nevida had not only broken every rule of decency. He had trampled on the code of the warrior seminary.

And no one protested. Most were taken with the sudden appearance of Mirnían, while a few clearly approved of Nevida's act.

With a stab of guilt and fear in his gut, Otchigen realized...

If Mirnían is here, where is Voran?

But he hadn't any time to follow that thought. He got up, the muscles in his legs tense, even quivering. He raised his right hand and drew breath to call a halt to the fight.

A fleshy hand, with only a vestige of former strength, squeezed his right shoulder.

Elder Pahomy, his five chins quivering, stood at Otchigen's right. He was a full head taller than Otchigen. Coupled with his immense girth, he was a sight that could shake the bravest warrior. The cohort elder shook his head. *Later,* his angry eyes seemed to say. Otchigen wasn't sure who would be the recipient of the elder's wrath—he himself, Nevida, or the entire third reach.

Otchigen's head darted back in the direction of the fight. For a shade of a moment, Karakul met Otchigen's glance. The eyes burned with joy. He wanted the dance to continue.

"Very well," said Otchigen to Elder Pahomy. "It's on *your* head, though."

"Do not crown a winner before his time," said Elder Pahomy. His voice was strained with the effort to keep down his anger.

For a brief moment, Otchigen remembered Pahomy in his youth—a lithe, deer-like fighter whose dance was deadlier than a snake's bite. What had happened to him? What had happened to all of them? With a sigh, Otchigen turned back to the fight that had been marred for him. Short of actually killing an opponent —an offense that would result in immediate execution, like a rabid dog being put down—Nevida could not have committed a worse crime in the eyes of the seminary. There was nothing noble in the continuation of such a battle, no matter how much Karakul seemed to thirst for it. It was a dirty thing.

This will taint all of us.

It was an unworthy thought, but like the lingering aftertaste of spoilt milk, Otchigen failed to purge it.

Nevida seemed to be winning now. He attacked with blinding speed, so fast that Otchigen could no longer anticipate his motions from the cues of his body. A lunge—Karakul bled from his arm. A perfect feint, disengage, slash, undercut—Karakul bled from two more places. A charge, then a leap back, then a punishing swipe on an overcommitted Karakul—the tide of the battle had turned the other way.

Otchigen forced himself to concentrate. Yes. Now he saw it. Although Karakul was bleeding from several livid gashes in both arms and in his left leg, his face was still as a pool of rainwater on a spring morning. More importantly, he still held his blade.

The peace seemed to radiate down into his fingers, which firmed with every second back into controlled grasps, into his elbows, which flowed like water again, unimpeded by jutting stones. And then his feet—they were hart's feet.

Nevida's mask of triumph slipped. In the shuddering of his weight-bearing leg, in the stripe of wet across his temples, in the barely-noticeable lowering of his blade's tip—he was terrified of Karakul.

Bad idea, idiot.

Karakul had seen it.

Then came Nevida's mistake. He overextended himself slightly. It was enough.

Otchigen held his breath in awe as Karakul, in spite of his wounds, counterattacked. In three quick slashes, he had Nevida on his heels. Otchigen had never seen such mastery with a blade. It wasn't taught. Karakul seemed possessed by a power of Aer.

Nevida's blade fell with a double clatter. It had broken in two. For a moment, Otchigen marveled at Karakul's powerful blow. But a twist in his stomach made him reconsider. No, nothing Karakul did would have broken Nevida's blade. It was an omen.

The ultimate dishonor. An omen of Adonais's divine displeasure.

The amphitheater groaned in mixed excitement and horror.

Nevida, at that moment, collapsed into a heap of flesh and tears. It was pitiful. It was shameful. It could not be borne.

"Get up, you filth!" cried Otchigen. "Get up! You shame your people with your self-pity! Up! Get up!"

The roar of the waterfalls rose in volume. Rose. Rose. Rose.

It was a thunder in his ears. He could almost feel the spray on his face.

Otchigen came back to himself, what seemed only a moment later.

Nevida's bloodied face lay in sand at Otchigen's feet. Blood dripped from Otchigen's lacerated knuckles. Somehow, he had ended up in the middle of the pentagon. How had he gotten there? Why was there blood on his hands?

Karakul's touch was like a summer thunderstorm that broke the heat into shards of hail.

"Lord, not this. Not this," he said, pulling him away.

Had he just beaten one of the boys?

He looked up in horror. All those eyes. They looked at him.

Mirnían was there too, in the pentagon. How had he gotten there so quickly?

With a look of both hatred and understanding, Mirnían turned away from Otchigen.

Mirnían stooped to help the shuddering Nevida up to his feet, who was still blubbering, spluttering something incomprehensible through a bloody mouth. Mirnían hushed him with a look and a hand around the shoulder. The prince's greenish tinge was gone, replaced by that forceful glance that could sway even the strongest heart. With a final look and a shake of the head, Mirnían turned Nevida toward the seminary and walked away.

CHAPTER 2
THE COLD HEARTH

Otchigen's heart beat so slowly that it seemed barely able to keep him alive. He lumbered through the palace forecourt—another pentagon, but this one larger, stone-flagged, filled with tight knots of brightly-dressed courtiers and black-robed cohort elders gathered higgledy-piggledy in a constant half-dance. They reminded Otchigen of marionettes on a storyteller's stage. It took an effort of will for him *not* to think they were all looking at him, or at least whispering about him. To distract himself, he tried to imagine the feast in the Dar's hall going on without him.

There would be long tables, garlanded and bedecked in towering creations almost too fanciful to eat—baked pies made to look like leaping stags, filled with twelve layers of delicacies like swan, saffron-spiced boar, perch, pike, even mountain goat. The aromas of the cinnamon-tinged mead tickled his memory. Maybe there would even be braggot from Karila to commemorate Karakul's victory. Just thinking of its sour-sweet taste made the back of his tongue curdle with anticipation.

And he would miss it all.

Though the food was only a small part of it. What he would miss most was the stirring warmth in the chest as the singing began after the fourth or fifth goblet, an invisible golden thread uniting all the men under the Dar's roof into a single unit, a brotherhood, a family. It was a feeling no less intense than the love between him and Aglaia.

Or at least their love as it had been only a few years before.

But that way lay confusion and darkness. Better to think of the grainy consistency of the granite flagstones under his feet.

For some reason, the wrought iron of the palace gates commanded his attention. Something about them was different today. Perhaps it was the heaviness of their black sheen, which seemed a bright, happy color compared to the numbness in his chest. Or maybe some mystery hid in the leaf-work interwoven with fine abstractions of sea beasts, mountain eagles, and fanciful chimaeras. There was one creature in particular—a raven in flight with a man's face and a beak instead of a nose—that allured and revolted him at the same time.

He tore his eyes away and almost tripped over the guards at the gates. They didn't turn to look at him, though their lowered face guards could have hidden any sarcastic expression well enough.

It was his imagination, surely. But he'd thought that he had heard a kind of music when he contemplated that raven-figure. A sinuous, alluring dance music, something that might be played on a viol, accompanied by a drum with a steadily increasing beat. A music that, once it took hold of you, would make you dance until you fell from exhaustion, and even then, it might force you to dance on.

Why in the Heights did I think of that?

He was hardly a musical man. That was his elfin daughter Lebía's area of interest.

Again, the thought whispered in his ear, nibbling at it like a rat in a cellar: "*You are going mad, Otchigen.*"

He hardly looked up from the rest of the cobblestoned road, trudging from the palace to his family's ancestral home. It crowned the highest mound of the third reach of Vasyllia. He felt, more than saw, the looming shapes of two- and three-story wooden mansions, each with windows and eaves carved no less fancifully than the gates of the palace. Even when the houses stood long distances away from the main road that wound through the hanging gardens of the third reach, he felt them as though the windows were eyes, each pair more judgmental than the next.

With disgust at his own morbidity, he forced himself to consider the one constant in his life. His hearth. The ancient symbol of married love. Yes, it *was* true that in recent months Aglaia had not been herself and had let the orderliness of the house slip a bit. One day it might be dinner offered half an hour later than usual. Just last week, she had forgotten to give him his cup of smoky tea before the storytelling at the hearth on the night of Temple. That had annoyed him, but he had not let it show. Not too much. Or the day Voran was to start the Ordeal of Silence, a day when he had made it clear that every room should shine in cleanliness. The state of the dinner table that evening was... well, Aglaia did complain of a headache that evening.

Come to think of it, she had been complaining of aches and pains for a long time now. Fah! She was always prey to such fancies. Otchigen was sure that if she wanted it strongly enough, she would be well in a day. One good night of sleep, one day of leaving things to the servants, not controlling their every move, one day in the fresh mountain air—she would be good as new, he knew it.

He approached the cherry groves that surrounded his estate. The trees were blushing and frothing with white flowers edged in pink. The closer he came, the more their subtle, sweet fragrance wove itself into the ever-present smell of mountain pine and the freshness of the falls, closer here than in the palace. Every once in a while, teasing like a lover, the smoke from his kitchen topped it all. The smells suffused him with peace, even more than usual. He thought he heard the clanging of cutlery and the creaking of the spit—partridge, perhaps, or maybe even game hens with that berry wine sauce he loved so much.

He nearly ran through the terraced back garden, where the tomatoes were only just beginning to flower, and the trailing cucumbers were already reaching their tendrils around the wooden stakes placed in the loamy earth. Oh, how he wanted to bite that first ripe tomato, to salt it, to drink it down with sour ale. But they were still green and puny. He would have to content himself with the goblet of wine that Aglaia would surely have ready for him. She knew he would be tired. She had probably not heard of his... mistake... in the pentagon. But she was sure to feel his distress from afar. She always did on such days, when nothing went as it should, when the perfection of the day's order collapsed in chaos around him.

The door to the house was locked.

That was strange. Surely Aglaia, or any of the servants for that matter, would have known that he preferred to come home the back way. It was an unspoken rule that everyone abided by.

They're not expecting me home for at least another hour. Yes, that must be it.

He beat on the door with his fist.

Nothing happened.

He beat again, more loudly this time.

Something crashed far inside, then he heard the unmistakable voice of Her Lardship Verina—the best cook in Vasyllia, who, contrary to all expectations and, indeed, her own nickname, was skinny as a stalk of barley. Her voice barked, more strident than usual, growing louder with every second.

Surely Her Lardship won't open the door herself. What are the maids and manservants for, then?

It *was* Her Lardship who opened the door. Her face, which was red from anger, flashed white when she saw him. Normally, that sort of quick shift in her face would have made him laugh, but his anger was beyond simmering now. It was all he could do to keep his voice calm.

"My dear Verina, what in Adonais's holy name are you doing opening the back door?"

She spluttered, her mouth opened, but nothing but a croak came out.

Otchigen's mouth twisted into a knot that matched the two larger ones forming in his shoulders.

"What is going on? Something's wrong, isn't it?"

"Wrong?" Her voice came back, but it cracked as it did. "No more than usual. Not since…"

"Is my lady taken to her bed *again*?"

A strange expression flitted across Her Lardship's face. Otchigen didn't recognize it. It may have been… sorrow? She was never anything but determined and single-mindedly unswerving. What was going on in his own house?

"This is ridiculous." He said it more for himself than the cook, and felt abashed immediately. He stepped past her into the damp, pleasant coolness of the wine cellar. "Well, I'll deal with it later. Come, since you're here, you must take a flagon of my father's best. Today is a day for celebration." His heart pinched at the memory of Nevida's bloody face. He winced. "A celebration. We have a new champion at the seminary. And do you know who, Verina? Karakul! I told you, didn't I? I told you he'd be the one…" He turned around, but Her Lardship wasn't following him. She still stood at the doorway, staring at him with an expression he couldn't see because of the sunlight behind her. "Are you even listening to me, Verina?"

"Are you listening to yourself? You're chattering like a fifteen-year-old girl. Are you even aware of what's going on in your house?" That tone he knew. Chilling disapproval. He knew how to deal with it.

"Yes, yes, Verina, you've always been the expert on all things *outside* the kitchen as well as within it. But what you couldn't possibly—"

She actually interrupted him. "Don't use that tone with me. Not today. Not when your lady…*your lady!*"

She burst into tears and ran past him back into the kitchen.

"Verina, the wine!" Surely, she was overreacting. He had seen Aglaia that morning before he left. She was a bit pale, yes, but she hadn't slept well. All easy enough to explain. "Never mind. I'll get it myself."

In rising anger, Otchigen walked through the open doorway into the long hearth-hall, the center of the house, and in many ways the center of his heart. Here, he lounged every evening in a specially-made rocking chair carved from birch. Here he had rocked Lebía to sleep every night when she was a small thing that hardly fit across his forearm. Here he told tales every Temple night as the hearth-fire played with the shadows thrown back by the carved pillars holding up the lofts of the second story, making every shadow into a monster or a hero or a Sirin in flight.

The hearth was cold. The wood was frosted over with day-old ash. There was dust on the columns.

The servants had not lit the hearth since last night.

That was the final straw.

CHAPTER 3
A STRONG WOMAN

Aglaia lay in their shared bed, which was raised above the ground on four posts—a rare innovation among the Vasylli. She was in her night-shift of pale linen, propped up with what looked like every single pillow in the house. Her hair wasn't done. It flowed down her shoulders in an oily mess, framing her face. She did look worse than this morning. The livid spots on her cheek hadn't been there before.

She turned her dark eyes at him. They had nothing of sickness in them. Only the stubborn patience of a wife who is about to listen to a litany of complaints from a peevish husband.

Every time. Every time he recognized that she knew what was coming. Every time his heart prompted him to calm himself, to let things be. But no. Every time, the fire in his chest got the better of him.

How dare she look at me like that? Doesn't she know? Doesn't she understand the stresses of life as a Voyevoda, the right hand of the Dar?

He needed no preamble. Her eyes let him know that she had already conducted the preliminary part of the conversation in her own thoughts.

"Do I ask so much of you, my love?" Though he was sure of the answer, he didn't stop to hear it. "Am I one of those boorish third-reacher husbands who expect their wives to be in the kitchen with the cooks at all hours of the day, who demand things to be done on a schedule, who never let their wives outside the sewing room? I am a generous husband. A loving husband. Am I not?"

"You are, my husband." There was hardly a pause in the middle of that phase, so he wasn't sure if she was agreeing with him or merely admitting the fact of their marriage. It pricked him and goaded him on.

"You know what an important day this is. Not for me only. It's not my comfort I'm talking about here. It's the day. On this day, of all days, was it so hard to ask the servants to bring the house at least to some semblance of order?"

"Otchigen, they were with me all morning. And I didn't expect you for another—"

"You know well enough you wouldn't have managed to get it all ready in time. You needed the entire morning to bring things merely back to normal! And what if I had brought back someone from the seminary with me?"

"You're right, my love. It's my fault. I—"

"I only want a few things, you know that. How many times..." He sighed as his heart constricted in a vise. They began so many of their arguments like this. It was almost pointless to continue. But the thorn pricking him wouldn't allow him to stop. "You know how I am after a day at the seminary. I only want a few things. A bit of food. A warm hearth. A door that isn't shut and locked against its master as though he were a common thief." The memory of the cellar door being locked only stoked the fire in his chest. If only his hearth was half as large as that fire...

"Is that true, Verina?" asked Aglaia placidly, her manner unruffled, as it always was during their arguments. Verina almost crawled from the doorway where she had been standing, half-concealed.

"Yes, lady. It's my fault."

"Can we please have this conversation without any servants?"

Otchigen's voice rose in pitch with every word, until he was almost barking the last word.

Aglaia's eyes went round, and she breathed deeply. He knew that reaction as well. This was not going to be a good conversation.

When Verina and the maid had gone, Otchigen began pacing back and forth, kicking up the fresh rushes on the floor as he went. With the corner of his eyes, he noticed an unfamiliar brass basin by her bed, filled with some kind of liquid. He turned around and didn't give it another thought. Finally, when the fire inside him was like a lightning bolt, he turned to her, looming over her.

"Don't you love me? I give my life to you. I am always ready to give you anything you need. I've always tried to anticipate your needs even before you see them yourself. Have you forgotten the second-day dress?" It was their own private joke. Whenever he felt particularly generous or wanted to help around the house, he would ask her to wear the dress she wore the day after their wedding. It was a dress spectacularly unsuited to any housework. She could hardly move in it, it had so much gold thread in it. He would ceremoniously seat her on his own rocking chair, bring her tea, and rub her feet. "Well? You haven't had a chance to put it on in the last few months? Is that it?"

She almost rolled her eyes, but stopped herself. He was too far ahead of himself to react.

"All I ask is a few things, you know that. On this day, of all days, could you not have—"

"Otchigen, my love." The accent on the word "love" was filled with years upon years of long-suffering. It made him even more angry. "I am not well. It's worse today. Verina even—"

"Aglaia, you are such a strong woman. Cannot you just..." He wanted to say it aloud. Something prevented him.

Aglaia's brows were drawn together and she hunched over slightly, her eyes inward and distant. Otchigen immediately felt guilty.

"I'm sorry, my love. You know I want the best for you, yes? I've already had the best doctors, the Dar's own leech. You know they say that there's nothing wrong with your body. All you need is—"

"Don't tell me what I need." Her voice cracked like a whip. His heart plunged at the emotion behind her words. There was something foreign there. Had they really grown so far apart?

"I only want..."

"It's not about what you want, Otchigen. If you think I'm inventing an illness for my own feminine reasons—you'd be mad to think it—but go ahead and say it." The accent on the word "feminine" dripped with irony. He could hardly recognize his wife in that tone.

He wanted to say it. Terribly. Every muscle in his body clenched in his desire to say it.

He did not say it.

"Otchigen, what will it take for you to believe your own wife? I am very ill."

He sighed, but said nothing. He sat on the bed, but felt her recoil from him.

The silence grew between them like a rent in the earth that formed after an earthquake. She seemed to be struggling with something. Nodding suddenly, as though she had reached some fateful decision, she began to undo the clasps of her linen shift.

"What are you doing?" Otchigen jumped up with the swiftness of his younger self. "I don't want to..."

Her look silenced him. Usually, that look had an edge of irony that could diffuse all his bluster. But it wasn't there today.

She continued undoing her shift and revealed the upper part of her chest. It had reddish spots, almost lesions, on it. Then she raised her sleeves. The same strange lesions marked both arms all the way to the elbow.

So now she had taken to burning herself with hot irons? Was this some kind of ancient, heathen healing practice?

"Is it like those... what are they? Mustard wraps?" he asked, not able to keep the disdain from his voice.

Something in her eyes died. That was the only way he could explain it to himself. And he realized what a blunder he had made.

"My love, I didn't realize—"

"No," she said, in an expression of such profound despair that he wanted to claw his own eyes out. "You haven't realized much of anything these past..."

She let it fade away. Then she turned away from him, hugging herself.

He reached a hand to her, wanting to caress her, to take her in his arms, to kiss her, to promise her everything would be well, that they were one person, not two, that they could weather any storm...

But he didn't.

He turned away from her, sighed, and walked out of the room.

◈

HE STOPPED, his body shivering in the aftermath of the fire in his chest, and stared at the still-cold hearth-hall. The bear-head carvings that joined the vaulted roof to the columns snarled at him with a hint of laughter. The hole in the ceiling, which some idiot artist in his grandfather's employ had decided should look like the sun, looked more like an accusing eye. He had never understood the artist's intention. There were rays painted in cracking gold and vermillion extending outward from the opening. But the effect was never achieved, because the house was built in such a way that the mountain headwall prevented the sun from ever shining from that direction.

Another failure for a moribund house, he thought.

The servants scurried all over the room—either like rats or like beetles, he couldn't decide which—picking up bits of refuse, dusting the corners, trying to light some kind of fire in the hearth, which for the life of it wouldn't light. As soon as the fire in his chest went out, every fiber of his body's muscles felt leaden. He lurched toward his rocking chair, holding on to its back for a moment, considering whether to sit or not.

The fire in his chest having faded, as it always did, it left behind a gaping abyss that ached to be filled with anything. But nothing would fit in it. It was hungry, insatiable. Excuses for his behavior welled up in his mind, but they tumbled into the abyss in his chest and disappeared, leaving only heaviness in his limbs and numbness in his mind.

He sat down with a groan. The chair creaked, as though complaining of his bulk. One of the servants brought the flagon of wine he had brought up from the cellars himself, placing it on the four-legged table that sat just at his right elbow, perfect for plates of food and cups to be reached easily, without any exertion.

Wine? Now? Have all the servants lost their minds?

With a barely-suppressed roar, he hurled the table, the flagon, and the wine across the room. It shattered as brilliantly in the light of the sputtering hearth as a shower of falling stars on a clear winter night.

The servant, sobbing quietly, ran away.

Otchigen didn't even have the energy to call her back to clean up his mess.

What a mess he had made.

Aglaia was sick. Very sick. He should have known it. Why had he persisted in his stupidity? Why had he thought it was just a plea for attention or a feminine fancy or... something? He didn't seem to know which way was up anymore. His thoughts rattled in his mind like rabid dogs in a cage, heedless of the wounds they received every time they threw their bodies against the bars. He wanted to sleep. He wanted to forget.

But the abyss in his chest kept eating and eating, leaving behind nothing but the guilt, the heaviness.

He didn't even rock the chair, staying still as death. He had acted. Look where that had gotten him. She was sick; she needed rest. He had probably exhausted her to her limit. Oh, why was he such a thick-skulled fool? His own darling wife! His own beloved lady!

He moaned.

A slight creak across the hall roused him. It wasn't the servants. It was someone trying not to be seen.

"Is that you, Lebía?" he whispered, as he would to a skittish deer that he wanted to feed from his hand.

A shadow twitched across the hall, between two of the central pillars. The bears holding those columns didn't sneer. They seemed to be mourning. The crouched-over shadow rocked back and forth, softly crying.

"My girl, please, come here. Come to me." Otchigen rose so clumsily that the rocking chair fell backward and clattered on the ground, overturning another table with a candlestick on it, adding to the general racket.

The shadow jumped in terror and ran away. Otchigen had just enough time to see the disheveled head of his eight-year-old daughter as she fled from her own father, as though he were a monster.

"Lebía, I'm your father! Come back here at once."

There was no answer. Only a door opening and slamming shut somewhere on the other side of the house.

Otchigen, like a marionette with its strings suddenly sheared, fell in a heap against the wall. A tapestry twisted uncomfortably behind him. He turned around to see the mounted figure of a Vasylli warrior baring steel at a writhing serpent under his piebald steed's upraised hoof.

"I have always sought to be that warrior," he said to himself aloud. "The ideal of manly virtue. To allow the idea of Vasyllia to be reflected, however poorly, in my efforts. But have I stooped to the serpent's level today?"

"My Lord Otchigen!"

It was an unfamiliar voice, at least at first. Otchigen had never heard it in the comfort of his own home. As he turned to find the speaker, he placed the voice. It was Rogdai, one of the wardens of the main gates of Vasyllia. A bearded swordsman, head uncovered, his black and gold livery smeared with grease and badly wrinkled. At Otchigen's look, his face twisted into an abashed sneer, the kind of subservient, insinuating look that Otchigen deplored. He knew Rodgai's type. Never one to do anything more than the minimum of what was expected of him. Not a true warrior, he.

"Yes?" Otchigen asked, feeling the stiffness of his no longer young body. "What is it?"

"The Dar requests your presence. There's been an embassy from Karila. Something about an omen. And an army of nomads amassing in the Steppelands."

CHAPTER 4

THE RUSTED BLADE

Otchigen didn't bother to change. He was already in his ceremonial best, though his clothes seemed to have gone through the same ordeal his soul had undergone during this past day. The golden embroidery of suns and moons and stars on the pale grey silk looked more like faded copper wire. He considered putting on a cloak edged in the ermine of his office but, even in the evening, the heat was oppressive, as though the air itself had fled to the wine cellars to wait for night.

As he walked out his front entrance, he was struck dumb by the sunset. The summer sky was streaked with bands of clouds that darkened in color from pale orange to wine-red the farther they rose from the far line of peaks which served Vasyllia instead of a horizon. The air just above him pulsed with darkness, as though a great beast were pushing down toward the mountain ridges, waiting for night to overwhelm Vasyllia. Only the flickering flames on the Covenant Tree, barely visible in the Temple Plain far below him in the first reach, sought to push that darkness back. But the white flames on the aspen sapling were low. Soon it would be the time for the annual Summoning of Fire, when the priests invoked fire from the Heights as pledge of the continuation of the Covenant between the creator

Adonais and Vasyllia. Until then, it seemed that Vasyllia was vulnerable.

"My Lord Otchigen? Shall we?" Rogdai waited amid the flowering cherries, his face indistinct in the evening murk.

You wait on my convenience, soldier, not the other way around. Otchigen's thought was almost accompanied by a growl, but he managed to stop it in time. The sunset, as though in concert with his darkening mood, lost its luster. It was nothing more than a few clouds in a darkling sky. Nothing ominous. Nothing to wonder at.

To Otchigen's surprise, Rogdai led him through the palace, past the Dar's personal tower, to the Chamber of Counsel. It was unusual for the Dar to use that room without the Dumar, the forty self-important representatives of the three reaches of Vasyllia, in attendance. But surely the Dumar would not need to be summoned for a report from an ambassador. Especially from Karila.

At that thought, his face flushed with embarrassment. How could he still think so little of Karila? Especially after it had given Vasyllia a champion for the ages?

Dim and colorless was the fresco of the Covenant Tree on the far wall, meeting the ceiling at a sharp peak. No light filtered through the multi-colored glass windows. The only light in the room came from three braziers near the thrones at the far end of the hall. Dark shadows cavorted along the empty galleries of dark-stained wood where the Dumar usually sat in attendance. The Dar's throne of white marble was strangely empty. For a moment, Otchigen even stopped walking, fearing that he had been led into some sort of a trap. But his good sense came back when he saw that Dar Antomír sat on the lower seat of malachite, usually reserved for Prince Mirnían.

So, this was a very informal meeting, after all. Why had Rogdai suggested it was so urgent?

Then Otchigen came close enough to see the Dar's face, and he redoubled his pace.

Dar Antomír looked as though he had aged ten years in a day. He was no young man at sixty-seven years of age, but he had always been youthful. One of those who age early but then don't change in appearance for the next forty or fifty years. He had always had a back like an iron pike, the corded muscles in his neck hinting at what must be a warrior's body, even in his twilight years. But what had always astounded newcomers were his eyes. They were almost ice blue, though soft and gentle, and they laughed even when his overly bushy brows met in the middle of his forehead. They were not so much young as ageless. It was no wonder that some of the first-reachers actually believed that he would live forever, ushering Vasyllia into a legendary golden age.

But now, his eyes had actually changed color. Or rather, they seemed to have lost the blue. They were grey, made all the drabber by the sharp red of the several spots in the whites of his eyes. Though he sat with his back propped against hard stone, he stooped. This was a different man.

What could have wrought such a change overnight?

"Ah, my dear friend. Good to see that you... are yourself again."

The Dar's voice strained barely perceptibly. Where was the usual spark of joy at seeing Otchigen? Where was the implicit endless well of shared memories of camaraderie and warrior intimacy?

With a plunge of his heart into his gut, Otchigen realized that his misdeed at the testing of the warriors was probably at least partially at fault for the Dar's distress. But surely not for the sudden aging?

At the foot of the dais stood a nondescript man in a dark kaftan cinched with a multi-colored woven rope. He turned his head only toward Otchigen. The same round face, flat features, and angled eyes that Karakul boasted, but with a full, dark beard streaked with white. His eyes were nothing like Karakul's brilliant hazel. These were brown like slabs of dusty stone. In fact, everything about him was almost calculated to mislead the eye into thinking that he was not worth anyone's notice.

"My sword and my heart are yours, Highness," said Otchigen formally, surprised at the hoarseness of his voice. He fell to his right knee and bowed his chin to his chest. "Though unworthy, I crave the Dar's love and honor his call."

"We can talk about your unworthiness later," said a different voice from the half-darkness to the Dar's right. It was reedy and nasal. With a gurgle of disgust in the pit of his stomach, Otchigen recognized the willowy and dark-bearded figure of Kalun, the chief priest of Adonais. Obsessed with external piety, condescending in his manner even to the Dar, he was possibly Otchigen's least favorite person in Vasyllia. After Nevida, that is.

"Not now, Otar Kalun," said Antomír with a brief flash of his usual liveliness. "I need Otchigen's council. You are here as a courtesy, and to witness."

The cleric's face darkened visibly, even in the smoky light of the braziers. Otchigen chortled into his nose, just loud enough to be heard. Kalun pretended not to hear a thing, though the flush of crimson across his high cheekbones was evidence enough of his excellent hearing.

"Otchigen!" the Dar snapped into his military-command voice. Otchigen responded instinctively by freezing in place and slapping his hand on the hilt of his longsword. "This is Sagyn-duk. Our father appointed him Special Envoy to Vasyllia from the Karilans."

"Your father?" Otchigen goggled. The man didn't look older than forty. But to be of Dar Mirolov's reign... He would have to be eighty years old at least. What was going on here? There was something he wasn't being told. "Highness. Am I to understand that all Karilans enjoy such blessed longevity?"

Antomír barked a laugh, and in that brief moment, he was himself again. But anxiety reasserted itself in the body of his friend almost instantly.

"No, my dear friend. I did say *Special* Envoy, did I not?"

The emphasis was significant, though at first Otchigen was flummoxed by it. Something he was supposed to remember, something important. Something secret and dangerous.

Then it came back to him. Immediately, he felt the blood drain from his face.

"Has it been stolen then?" his voice was hushed, but more from strain than the lack of it. "Vohin Rodgai said something about nomad armies in the Steppes?"

"No, it has not been stolen," said the man named Sagynduk in a thick Karila accent. His voice was even younger than his body and higher pitched than Otchigen expected. Resonant. Like a horn to Antomír's deep bell-like bass. "Much worse. It has rusted through."

Otchigen's eyelids opened wide involuntarily. With a rush of excitement, he tasted the war-wind. How good it would be to face an enemy again. It had been too long. With a deep breath, he focused into his war-awareness.

"Special Envoy to Vasyllia"—the name was a bit of a joke, though the person himself was anything but. He never came to Vasyllia, never left Karila. No one in Karila even knew what he did, though the ruling council of Karila honored him even more than the noble families, even more than the families of clerics and healers, who were especially honored in Karila above all other cities. He was the keeper of the greatest bond between Karila and Vasyllia. In fact, it was probably the only thing that kept Karila from consummating its ever-present desire for independence from the hegemony of Vasyllia.

This bond was a sword—ancient, long-bladed in the Vasylli manner, and in all respects perfect. Legends held that it was given to Lassar, unifier of the Three Cities and blessed ally of the Harbinger, by that High Being on the occasion of the swearing of Covenant between Vasyllia and the Heights of Aer. Vasyllia received proof of the Covenant in the form of the flaming sapling whose fire never died, ever fed by the annual Summoning of Fire from the Heights. Karila received the Blade of Covenant, and it was said that while the blade remained in Karila, untouched, no war would touch Karila.

And so it had been.

If the blade had rusted, it could mean that Karila would try to separate itself from the Brotherhood of Cities. And that meant war between Vasyllia and Karila. Otchigen's excitement cooled when he realized that if that were to happen, Karakul would certainly fight against Vasyllia. They might even meet in open battle. Otchigen's enthusiasm for the war-wind died down considerably at that thought.

"So the blade is of human provenance after all," said Kalun in a voice as though he were trying to hide a guilty pleasure. "So much for the legends."

Sagynduk spat at the cleric's foot. Everyone froze in shock, even the Dar.

"Blasphemy, even from the mouth of a man called Otar, is still blasphemy."

Kalun's entire body seemed ready to lunge at the diminutive Karilan.

"Sagynduk, perhaps you have—" began the Dar.

"I am old, Highness. And now I smell the dung of my years. No time for... ceremony." He gave the last word all the disdain his slight figure could muster. "Far has Vasyllia fallen indeed, if her Father-Otar does not recall the prophecy of the Harbinger to the Karila.

'Bright is the blade, and sharp the edge
Of love and honor between souls.
But rusted blade shall be the sign
That Covenant's last hour tolls.'"

Otchigen had never heard that particular prophecy. He doubted that it was written down in *The Sayings* at all. Kalun's bemused face seemed to confirm his suspicion.

"I do not doubt your word, Sagynduk," said the Dar carefully. "But my friend Otchigen may. And I rely on his wisdom, sometimes more than on my own."

The rest remained unsaid. Otchigen knew that the Dar placed some sort of vast hope on his shoulders.

If only he knew what to say.

"Sagynduk...Forgive me, I do not know the proper honorific..."

Sagynduk looked ready to spit again, and his eyes blazed. Otchigen was reminded of Karakul's inner fire, and he decided that he liked this strange man. Spitting and all.

"Who am I to doubt the word of an Envoy, of one on whom the Harbinger's word lies heavily," Otchigen said, with an attempt at the pattern of speech that Karakul had tried to teach him once. The way a commoner might speak to a priest. It was the highest honor he could offer to the strange man.

Sagynduk's mouth twitched briefly. It was the only indication that he smiled. Otchigen considered it enough encouragement to go on.

"Your coming to the Mother of Cities cannot sit easily on your back. Not with your burden, never to be lain down. Tell me, is it the rusted blade alone that troubles your peace, or did I hear rumors of war? A nomad army in the Steppes?"

He couldn't help that a note of incredulity crept into the last sentence. The mere suggestion that any nomad chieftain could ever stop fighting his own family members long enough to actually gather a war party, much less an army, was laughably ridiculous.

Sagynduk looked into Otchigen's eyes for a long time. As he did, his own blazing eyes softened, and something like pity seemed to simmer deep inside them. Otchigen began to twitch under their long scrutiny.

"It would be unheard-of, I agree. But the rumors persist. Not a week passes that a merchant does not return to Karila with half his wares stolen, dark stories of armies massing among uniting clans. But that may be nothing more than gossip. What I do know is that the Ruling Council of the Seven, I tell you this in all confidence, is on the brink of declaring martial law. If that happens..."

"Then they will break the alliance with Vasyllia." The Dar finished the sentence for him.

It was part of the old agreement between city-states. Only Vasyllia had the right to declare martial law for any of the Three Cities.

"What if Vasyllia pledges her own armies to fight this nomad danger?" Otchigen asked.

"We would need incontrovertible proof," the Dar said doubtfully. "Judging by everything you have already told me, I would not send anyone to Karila. You will forgive me, Sagynduk, but it sounds like your city is merely chafing at her collar. Would you suggest that your people have just found an excuse for something they have desired for a long time?"

"You mean separation from the so-called Brotherhood of Cities? I am no politician. But you may be right."

For a long time, no one said anything, every man lost in his own thoughts.

"What is it that the tales say?" said Otchigen, attempting a lighter tone. "The morning is wiser than the evening? Sagynduk is tired from his journey."

"Yes, of course," said Dar Antomír, visibly relieved. "The best steam room of the palace, a chamber of your own in my personal tower. You will dine with me as well, I insist."

Sagynduk looked about ready to explode into a tirade of contrary words, but he nodded placidly.

"We also have the old saying. The dawn is wiser than the night. Old wisdom for an old problem. It is proper."

"Good. Otchigen, you will stay?"

"Highness, I beg your leave. My wife..."

"Yes, I had heard, my friend. Forgive me. Give all my love to your lady. Tell her I await her wit and her beauty at my table as soon as she can bear spending an evening with an old bore."

CHAPTER 5
FIRES IN VASYLLIA

Rushing back and forth through the third reach, back and forth—it happened often enough since Otchigen's appointment as Voyevoda, chief warrior of the armies of the Mother of Cities. But today, more than ever before, the way stretched before him, endless and tiring. It was as though the moonlit path grew longer as he walked, not shorter. Otchigen cursed loudly, imprecating himself, the Heights, his extended family.

In such moods, it was better if he remained out of doors, away from the comforts of home. It would not take much to light the char-cloth in his chest, always dry and always ready to catch at the faintest spark.

Aglaia's expression as he misjudged the wounds on her body flashed through his memory. No, he did not dare spend even another minute away from her. Without realizing it, he had started running.

Each step of his booted feet sounded loud, even ponderous. Bell-like. Each step raised the dry dust of summer, and with it rose the foreboding in his gut, reaching for the abyss in his heart, filling it up.

Suddenly, lightning flashed, as though from a clear sky. But no, he remembered now. Burly grey-black clouds had been gathering all day, far taller than the mountains of Vasyllia, as though the Heights of Aer revealed themselves, greater and more terrible than the Vasyllia of earth. A second bolt flashed, and with it came the thunder, sounding to his beleaguered mind like the cracking open of every mountain peak in Vasyllia. A third bolt flashed, and he saw his estate in the distance, for a moment stark, as though it was on fire.

No. It *was* on fire.

Lightning flashed not one hundred paces from him. The shock of it knocked him off his feet. With a sound like the unmaking of creation, fire burst up from the ground to his right, on the lands of Sudar Gartanían. No, not just his lands. His house burned as well. Otchigen stopped in horror, turning about in place as the acrid smell of smoke reached him. Three houses—now it was five, not including his own—were burning like the beacon-fires on the border between Vasyllia and Nebesta.

What are you doing standing here, you idiot? Your house! Your family!

He bolted forward as the third reach came alive around him, people erupting in droves from the houses like ants from a collapsing anthill. Some called to him for help, but he looked nowhere but ahead, where he thought he could still see the stark outline of his own mansion burning in the flames.

Then the wind came.

It roared as though it were a ravenous mountain lion attacking a pack of wounded goats. The cries of the third reach rose with it, as any hope of stopping the fires was lost. Now all they could do was contain it as much as possible.

And yet, through all the chaos, through the screaming, through the flashes of lighting that blinded him for moments on end, he heard a whisper of a thought somewhere far away in the depths of his mind.

Your house was on fire before the lightning struck.

It was not his own thought, he was sure. It was suggested to him. But he had no doubt of its truth.

His feet hardly seemed to touch the path any more.

✺

BEFORE HE REACHED HOME, the rain came—a hot, summer downpour that together with the wind could break trees with its power. He was drenched in less time than it took to draw his sword. But the discomfort was only momentary, as he realized that the immediate danger of fire was past.

His realization was confirmed as he approached his two-story, three-gabled sprawling house that even from the ground looked like some huge dragon ready to pounce. The smoke from it rose, mixing with an evening mist that had come with the rain. Only one of the forelegs of the serpent—a wing added during his father's time to accommodate his grandmother's strange passion for clay pottery—was badly damaged. The rest of the house looked merely scorched, with some of the gilding on the eaves gone and one section of the roof slightly caved in. Quickly, he tried to guess which part of the house that was.

His stomach twisted. It was the bedroom he and Aglaia shared. He was sure of it.

As he came through the cherries, which were shedding pale blossoms in the rain as though the trees themselves were weeping with the heavens, he saw Lebía, wrapped in what looked like five heavy blankets, her hair sticking to her scalp. Her face was red and wet, and he suspected it was not only the rain that drenched it.

He scooped her into his arms even before she realized he was there, eliciting a yelp and a frenzied attempt to escape, followed soon after by a tight embrace. She had not hugged him like that in months. Now he was no longer sure his face was only wet from the rain, either.

"You're not hurt, Lebía?" he boomed, trying to make himself heard over the continuing din of the wind and the rain.

She shook her head, but then erupted into a fresh torrent of sobs.

"Papa, Papa. It's Mama. She's gone!"

⬥

THE HOURS that followed were little more than a series of sounds and images, barely joined together by anything other than the ever-present sense that the world was about to end. If not the whole world, at least his own. The door to the wine cellar, torn off its hinges. Her Lardship repeating, over and over again, "What will become of us?" Three young third-reachers caught in the act of trying to burn down Otchigen's house, tied roughly together and thrown like sacks of cabbages into the middle of the hearth-hall. Two menservants watching over them, armed with metal pokers. The whinny of a horse in fright. Lebía's huge eyes, red-rimmed from tears and fear.

Nowhere did he find Aglaia. Not a sight, sound, smell of her. No one knew where she was.

It was near dawn when he came back to his rational mind, awakening from some kind of stupor to find himself on his rocking chair, with Lebía sleeping in his arms like she used to when she was a baby. It was so domestic a scene, so perfect, that he turned to the front door, expecting to see Aglaia there with her quizzical half-smile, so redolent with yearning, holding a branch of the season's last rowan-berries. But the door was shut and barred. Its edges were still smoking.

He realized then that someone was speaking to him, and probably had been for a long time. He turned to the voice and realized, with some confusion, that it was Otar Gleb, a young priest only recently raised to the clerics from among the second reach. An ugly man, almost grotesquely so, with a misshapen nose and large eyes too closely placed together. The softness of his curling, blond hair—which would have looked beautiful on a young woman's head—only accentuated his ugliness.

"You may be inclined to blame yourself, I know," said Otar Gleb, his voice gentle and soothing. "But I do not. There is a place for that kind of ferocity in the fighters' pentagon. And Adonais knows that Nevida committed a breach that should, in all fairness, see him exiled to some pox-infested land on the far side of the Steppes."

With some effort, Otchigen remembered that they had been speaking for at least half an hour about the events of the past few days. They had only now begun speaking of the fires. Otar Gleb had brought news that only some of the fires had been naturally caused, while a few had been part of a plan by some friends of Nevida. A puerile act of revenge against Otchigen and the families who supported him in the Dumar.

"I think they were emboldened by the prince's support. That spiteful boy! And all because he didn't last the Ordeal, while my own Voran..." Otchigen couldn't finish the sentence. Voran had been inseparable from his mother. What would he do when he came out from the Ordeal?

"I'm sure Mirnían did what he thought was necessary." Otar Gleb smiled, and it was like a sunrise after a dark winter night. His ugliness softened, and his eyes shone. Otchigen had been wrong. Otar Gleb had his own kind of beauty. "Be sure to add it to your daily devotion, Otchigen, that you have the right—the grace, even—not to play both sides in a quarrel. Mirnían does not have that luxury."

Otchigen found himself at a loss for words, trying to untangle what he had imagined from what had actually happened. Otar Gleb leaned forward, his smile now no more than a dimple on each cheek.

"I understand that Lady Aglaia's disappearance is... not connected with the fires. That the servants had noticed her absence earlier in the day? At least we can be sure she did not perish in the flames. That is some comfort, no?"

It came back to Otchigen like a sudden wave that overwhelms and pulls under at the same time. Aglaia gone. Without a trace. As though she had simply vanished into thin air. No one had so much as seen a shadow of her since he had spoken to her that morning.

"Yes, Otar Gleb, I suppose you're right." Though nothing of the sort was true, of course. Naturally, her disappearance could have nothing to do with anything but the most important thing—their quarrel. "Though it's more of a comfort to Lebía, I imagine, not me. I will not be at peace until I have found her."

"You believe she has left then? Of her own volition? Or do you suspect foul play?"

The only foul play is my own.

"The circumstances of her disappearance are... strange, to say the least. I don't know what to believe any more, Otar. I only know I will not be capable of rational thought, much less a warrior's worth, until I find some word of her."

Otar Gleb nodded thoughtfully, but before he did, a very clear expression flashed across his face. It said a great deal, though it ended in a moment.

"You suspect I have done something to her?" Something of the growl returned to Otchigen's voice.

Otar Gleb's eyes opened in genuine surprise. "No, of course not! Though... I do imagine there are some who would suggest it. Even before you punished Nevida, you were unpopular with a certain kind of third-reacher family. But you already knew that."

Otchigen did. There was a worrying trend among some of the newer third-reacher families who had been raised to nobility for services performed for the Mother of Cities in the last hundred years or so. Most of them had a disturbing—and completely mercantile second-reacher—tendency to prefer cunning and compromise to honor and righteousness. He made it part of his daily responsibilities to extirpate those unworthy qualities, sometimes in public ways. He felt no qualms about it—

it was necessary for the virtue of the Mother of Cities. But they didn't appreciate the public nature of it.

"Well, Otar Gleb, I hope you will do what you can to stifle any sort of rumor. Especially when I am gone."

"Where will you go? Have you any indication of where she might have gone?"

"I have none. But there is one who may."

Otar Gleb smiled with genuine pleasure. "Ah! You go to have tea with the stylite. Excellent! Do give him my love, and tell him that I can smell his unwashed holiness all the way in the third reach."

CHAPTER 6

THE PILLAR-DWELLER

P ushing his shuddering legs those final few steps, Otchigen held his breath and leaned against the stout quarterstaff he held in his right hand, given him as a final blessing by the Dar himself. By this time, four days into his journey, calluses from the rubbing of the oak-wood had formed over the soft, blistery flesh—an embarrassing reminder of how much of a city-dweller he had become. Many were the days in his youth when he had spent weeks in the wild, hardening his body in preparation for an ordeal. Now, even his sword-hand had become soft. He hadn't realized it, not until these days in the wild. It made him think that perhaps he knew even less about himself than he thought he did.

Finally, he crested the peak. It had taken him most of the day to slog up this last rise. The footpath reached the cairn marking the summit, then twisted around it. Otchigen stopped for a moment to consider the cairn, then he fell on his knees before it and kissed the ground, closing his eyes and wrapping his fingers around the first stone that he happened to touch. As he rose, he placed the stone—a smooth pebble the size of his fist—on top of the cairn, making sure not to topple the entire structure.

This was the custom for any who would enter the valley of

the stylite. His name was Semyon, a strange hermit who lived on top of a pillar of stones he had crafted with his own two hands, probably more than fifty years ago. Though there were some in the first reach who swore by all that's holy that he had built that pillar over two hundred years ago. The story went that he had only come down from it once to visit Vasyllia in person. The reason for his visit was disputed, and the best version Otchigen heard was that he had taken violent offense at learning that Dar Antomír had canceled a rarely-celebrated, esoteric feast day honoring the dendrites of Cassían's reign.

Until he heard that story, Otchigen hadn't even known what a dendrite was. Thinking it was a species of river fish, he was astonished to find out that it was a kind of hermit who lived in the bole of a tree, never leaving it until he died.

However that may be, he did know for a fact that Dar Antomír, in his youth, had wanted to simplify the Temple Calendar, removing some of the less-attended feast days entirely or combining them into a single day of greater solemnity. He had done it with a few, but the Day of the Dendrites he had left alone.

Otchigen thought he understood the impulse that caused the hermit to abandon his pillar. He stood for the old order of the days of Covenant. He understood, as did so few Vasylli these days, that once you begin to undermine the traditions that had buttressed a civilization for centuries, even for perfectly logical reasons, you were laying cracks to the foundation of that civilization. If Otchigen had been in his place, he would have done more than simply come to Vasylli to voice his displeasure. He would have challenged someone to an open battle in the pentagon. The most ancient of rites—the ordeal by arms.

Perhaps he and the stylite would get along, after all.

Otchigen stopped to catch his breath, agog at the valley sprawling below him. The summer air that day had the peculiar quality—rare in other seasons—of giving everything in the distance a sheen of unreality. It was as though he looked at a very realistic fresco. The river snaking through the grassy valley, the tufts of willows on the banks of the river, the stands of alder and birch and aspen surrounding the crooked pillar of stone that looked like it would topple at any moment, and finally the hovel made of sticks, bark, and moss on the top of it—it all looked too concocted to be real. As though he could extend his hand to it all, and it would ripple away under his touch like a reflection in water.

Instead of wiping away the view, he started the steep way down—it was half footpath and half broken-down staircase from some lost age when such things were actually carved into the mountains.

As an entirely new group of muscles began to complain at the strain of the descent, Otchigen wondered if he hadn't made a mistake coming to Semyon.

The stories about him were varied in the most spectacular ways. Some said he was a kind, gentle soul who spoke little, and when he did it was all nonsense anyway. Others insisted on his spectacularly bad character as the reason for his living so far away from everyone. The one common thread in all the tales was his clairvoyance. And that vision was what Otchigen needed. To know where Aglaia was, no matter how far away.

He had spoken to the infrequent travelers on the Dar's road and the even more reclusive woodsmen living along the foot-paths—none had offered up any information as to the possible whereabouts of Lady Aglaia. None had so much as heard of a fine Vasylli lady traveling outside the city. What would a fine lady like she be doing out in the summer heat anyway, they wondered? And a few of them had turned away from Otchigen with doubting looks that seemed to suggest that perhaps it was better for the lady that this hulking shadow of a man would not find her, after all.

It was possible, he admitted to himself, that he imagined those looks. He trusted his senses and his impressions less and less. A foggy dimness often descended on his waking hours, so that he could walk for hours on end without realizing what sort of land lay around him. Once or twice he actually missed a cross-roads, forcing him to turn back and take the same road twice.

It worried him, but he tried not to think of it. It was becoming more and more difficult to think through anything. All he could hold in his mind clearly was Aglaia's pained face after their last argument. That was enough to force him to continue moving, even at night, when he should have been resting.

And so, as he approached the pillar of the stylite, he had to force himself to remember the exact words he had planned to use when speaking to the enigmatic hermit. From the many different versions of the tales, he had learned that upon a first visit, one must address Semyon as "Your Pillarliness." The second address could be either "great lord of the stones" or "great stone of the lords"—the accounts were confused as to which. But all agreed that a studied civility and conventionality in speech were necessary if the old man were to speak to you at all.

Something plopped against Otchigen's cheek. He felt it with his fingers and examined it. It was brown and it smelled foul. Otchigen stopped in mid-stride, shocked. Another gift came from above, landing on his left shoulder. He looked up at the top of the pillar.

"Just making you feel at home, my dear!" The screeched words came from a wizened old man with a beard so long it was tied in five knots just to keep it from tripping him. "I could be wrong, of course, but I believe you hark from the city of dung itself, no?"

"Your Pillarliness!" began Otchigen, but he could say no more. The old man had laughed so uproariously that he actually fell over and out of sight. Otchigen wondered if he had fallen off the pillar entirely.

"Pillarliness! Ho-ho-ho! Oh, that's good! Precious! The things the dung-heap-dwellers come up with these days!"

"I come from no dung heap," Otchigen said, his voice rising in annoyance. "I come from the Mother of Cities herself."

"The mother of shitties, more like!" And he cackled and hooted again. "I know why you've come. And I have no answers for you. Go home, raven-man. None of your blood-stained hands here! Your smell has preceded you for days. Blood and rot and filth. Go! Away with you!"

He disappeared.

Otchigen's mouth was open in utter shock. Though plenty of the stories described him as odd, none had said that Semyon was a madman. Still, the words he spoke echoed in his mind. If he hadn't known any better, he might have thought that the man spoke with the power of prophecy.

"Master, will you not at least tell me one thing? I will be on my way presently."

"One thing?" The hoary head popped into view again. "It was only one thing that led to the fall of Vasyllia. It was one thing only that caused the rotting rust to eat away at the relic of Karila. It was one thing alone that burned the fair lady of Nebesta to ashes. Or wait..." He cocked his head like a curious blue jay. "That hasn't happened yet, has it? Any of it?"

His eyebrows, bushy even from this distance, lowered so far down his brow that it seemed they might fall off his face entirely. He studied Otchigen, then his face softened.

"Not yet. No. And for all your stink..." He left the rest unsaid.

"Semyon!" Otchigen decided to discard all the stories and speak to this strange person man to man. "Surely you have loved a woman in your life. Surely you have felt the emptiness when she is lost. All I ask is information. A word. No more."

"Oh Heights! It's all so distressing sometimes. How does the Most High do it? All laid out before him, as on a tapestry, I imagine. A tapestry in constant motion, with every thread like a vein full of pulsing... events? Faces? How does he do it? I can hardly manage a shadow of it. Now for the poor creature. The poor wolf-woman."

Otchigen's patience was quickly reaching its end. Before he started screaming at this poor idiot of a man, he tried a last time.

"You may have heard from a traveler come to visit your holiness. The Lady Aglaia. Has she come here? Has anyone heard of her whereabouts?"

"Is it just an unbreakable inner focus? I have too much to scatter me, even here, even alone. If only there were some way to bore a hole in the Realms. Jump through it down into the Heights..."

The space inside Otchigen where the abyss gaped caught fire, and his fists clenched so hard he was sure he would find bloody marks from the nails on his palms.

"A pox on you! What Otar Gleb sees in you, I will never know. Though he was right about one thing. Your obsession with foul smells. He asked me to pass on his love, and to tell you that he smelled your unwashed holiness all the way from Vasyllia."

"Gleb! Oh, the rascal! He would say that, he would." And he laughed, but it was a sane laughter this time, with a note of a fully rational old man, a bit weary perhaps, but not mad. "It is good that you value his friendship, Otchigen. If you two lived in a different age, perhaps you might have found peace. But now..."

The face disappeared again for a time. It sounded as though he were rummaging though something in his hovel. Then Otchigen heard, to his surprise, the sound of scrabbling, as though someone were climbing up rock. Or *down*...

Surprised, Otchigen walked around the pillar. He saw Semyon climbing down the pillar with the skill of a mountain goat kid. He hardly looked down at all, as though his hands and feet knew exactly where the best ledges and holes were. In a few quick minutes, Otchigen was faced with a short, remarkably dirty old man whose holiness, as Gleb had said, if measured by magnitude of smell, was truly monumental.

"Yes, I know," said Semyon, sniffing loudly, then scratching his nose. "Well, not much time to wash if you know the end of the world is coming soon."

He said it with the same flippant tone as before, but then he seemed to notice something as he looked at Otchigen, and his eyes went a fraction wider than before. A slight movement, but Otchigen sensed that it revealed much. His tone from that moment was entirely serious, even commanding.

"Tell me, Voyevoda of Vasyllia. What sort of madness causes you to leave your hearth and your home right after a fire that could have wiped out the entire third reach of Vasyllia?"

"How do you...? So you *have* seen someone from Vasyllia, then? Did they have word of Aglaia?"

"Otchigen, tell me. Has anyone suggested to you that you are going mad?"

Something itched in Otchigen's chest, like a blind mole looking for soft spots in the earth to burrow. Otchigen didn't answer.

"No, I don't suppose anyone would brave that temper of yours. That thing you call warrior virtue." Semyon scoffed. "Warrior virtue indeed. A noble aspiration, but only if tempered. And not with your temper. So, madness. Yes, well, what else would you call it? The third reach burning, at least partially from the ill will of its own sons. A daughter with a broken heart, abandoned in hallways that still stink of smoke, without even her brother to look to her. A champion for the ages—your own words, I believe —in potential danger so obvious that a child could see it. And yet, you wander the wilds looking for the woman whom you drove out her own house yourself. Yes, I believe that is what you call madness."

Otchigen was so shocked by the exactness of Semyon's information that he forgot, for a moment, to be angry. By the time the mole in his chest had grown into a rat scrabbling for a way out of his chest, Semyon was speaking again.

"And the lapses in attention. The strange thoughts whispered in your ear, as though by another. Madness, I tell you. You are a danger to Aglaia. Why do you pursue her when it is so clear that she is better off without you?"

That was the final drop.

"I am not mad, pillar-dweller! Though I suppose if anyone were to suspect me of it, it would be someone as mad as you."

"It would indeed," said Semyon, his expression guarded, his eyes slitted as he watched Otchigen.

The rat in his chest was throwing itself madly against his ribs, biting, clawing, ripping its way out of him. How dare that old man suggest such a thing? Otchigen had been traveling for days on end seeking nothing but a bit of consolation. And this was what he was to receive? After so many years of unflagging service to his family, his nation, he was to be lectured in loyalty by a man who had abandoned the world to sit on top of a pillar and stare at nothing? This was unbearable.

Otchigen's hand shot out, grabbing the old man by the throat.

Break his windpipe!

The thought was so sudden, so sharp, so sweet on his mind, that Otchigen gasped. But he did not let go.

Semyon's face didn't change expression, even as it turned bluish-purple. His hands didn't come up to defend himself. He even seemed to smile a bit.

Break his neck!

Yes! I will! The foul canker on the earth's face. Deluding people with his words of so-called wisdom. The world would be lighter for his being taken off its surface.

Lebía's wet face flashed on his mind. Aglaia's expression of despair. Voran's calm, infuriating resolve. Karakul's laughing eyes.

With a groan that seemed to come from underneath him, from the rocks themselves, Otchigen dropped Semyon.

The old man tried to take a full breath, but it wouldn't come easily. As he twitched on the ground, looking like an overturned beetle trying to find its legs, he kept his eyes on Otchigen.

Finally, with a sound like a wooden spoon being dragged against a washboard, he breathed in fully and landed on his knees.

"Not madness, no," he wheezed. "Something else. Something that the great enemy desires. Your capacity to love, turned inward. Your powerful anger, turned outward. Two forces that, when linked, can break the world."

Otchigen, his hands shaking, fell onto his knees before the old man. Shuddering sobs had replaced the gnawing in his chest.

"I... forgive me... what happened to me? I've never..."

"Voyevoda of Vasyllia, can you see now? How you have made choice after choice that condemns not only you, but everyone who is attached to you? Can you not see that it is likely that Karakul is already dead? Killed in his own bed by his so-called brothers?"

"No... certainly things are not as bad as..."

"They are a great deal worse. You know this. You, of all men the most eager for the virtue of your city and its people. You, of all men most focused on your own honor and virtue. You, who have had such a tight control over your own thoughts and emotions that hardly a stray thought passed through you? And yet, who was it that beat Nevida to a pulp?"

"I don't ... I don't understand." A strange thought formed itself into words. "Am I the infection?"

"No, not you, my dear one. It is in Vasyllia, boring its way to the city's very bones. But it may be that you will carry it deeper still."

"But all I've ever wanted is the good of my ... You said it yourself..."

"If that were so, why do you abandon them all when you know full well that Aglaia is not only safe, she is better off where she is now? Away from Vasyllia. Away from the taint that infected her so badly that it broke through her skin in lesions."

His body shuddering sporadically, Otchigen fell on his knees. He hadn't considered it until this moment. Could his lapses in memory and Lebía's sickness both be expressions of a rottenness at the heart of Vasyllia? Was such a thing even possible?

"Something is going to happen to Vasyllia, isn't it? Semyon, tell me! What must I do?"

The stylite finally spoke without a wheeze as he stood up. Though he was a small man, he still loomed over the crouched figure of Otchigen.

"I am but a man. I see things, yes. And what I see is horrifying. If you go now, if you do not stop on your way home, you may —it is only just possible—delay the coming of the darkness to Vasyllia. But I do no know any more. Gamayun, the teller of all fates, sings to me in riddles, and the images in my dreams are soaked with blood and tears."

Otchigen, in a sudden flood of emotion that seemed to break every carefully crafted guard he had placed over his heart and mind over the many years of his military discipline, embraced the old man.

In that moment, he saw something that was not real. A flash of a scene so vivid, it left a trace on the back of his eyes, similar to the spots children see after they stare at the sun for longer than their parents allow.

It was this valley. The pillar had toppled. The body of the stylite was splayed out on one of the fallen stones. Thick metal pegs were driven into his hands and feet. His chest was slashed open.

Someone stood over the fallen stylite, holding the knife high as it dripped blood, dark in the fading light of an autumn sunset.

The man holding the knife was Otchigen himself, though he was emaciated, most of his hair had fallen out, and his expression was not his own.

"This event... I have seen it often over the years," said Semyon, banishing the vision. "I used to think that you did it willingly, for hatred of me." Otchigen let go of the old man as though he had splashed scalding water on him. "But now I think that you will no longer be in control of your own will at that moment. Know this, dear one. I have outlived even the span of life, even of the elder men of Lassar's day. And for one reason alone."

But he would not say what that reason was.

Otchigen, heedless of anything but his own terror, turned and ran.

I am my own man, he thought feverishly. *I have my own will. No one will take it. No one.*

CHAPTER 7

VORAN

O tchigen hardly stopped to rest at all on his way back to Vasyllia. Only when his legs buckled under him and his eyes closed, heavier than the lids on iron pots, did he simply fall over in place for a brief repose, sometimes on the path itself, sometimes a little way off it. He met no one, or at least didn't remember meeting anyone. He hardly noticed anything, need driving him to move forward. Occasionally, he thought he saw the sun glinting off the steel of a spear or a helm —perhaps a scouting party from Vasyllia or a merchant guard— but there was nothing more than the glint.

He was more and more sure that he was going mad.

When the first vista of Vasyllia opened up before him, he was shocked. At first, he believed it to be a delusion. He had not even realized at what point he had left the woodmen's paths and rejoined the Dar's road. And yet, there it was. And it grew nearer with each leaden step.

As he approached the plateau stretching before the great mountain city, bursting with the green of new growth and the foaming heads of wheat, more and more of his perception returned to him. His sour stomach twisted hungrily with each step, and he was shocked to find that his breeches hung loosely on him, as did his travel tunic. Had he eaten so little during his journey? His legs ached so deeply that he thought his bones might shatter at a breath of wind. His back groaned, twisted into a bent-forward shape that his military training decried. Even his fingers looked more like weathered wood than the muscular, veiny hands that had been smeared with Nevida's blood only a week ago.

With the return of his body's sensations came a storm of jumbled thoughts, as though they had been held back by a feeble dam that had only just collapsed.

They rushed over him so fast that he couldn't hold on to a single one of them. Instead, he focused his attention on the silvery path through barley fields leading directly to the twin gates of Vasyllia, set within an arch of marble carved to resemble two trees leaning toward each other to embrace at the point just above the peak of the gates. It was still early morning, so he was surprised to see the gates open ahead of him as he approached. Already carts full of wares were making their way back to Karila on the Dar's road. The merchants and their serving men hardly paid him any attention as he walked. Only a few of them seemed confused when they looked at the sword hanging on his hip. One of them had eyes that kept darting back and forth between Otchigen's face and his sword. Only on the third pass up and down did recognition come to his eyes. But it was a shocked recognition, nothing warm or familiar about it.

They think I have something to do with my wife's disappearance.

The thought made him laugh bitterly.

"You there! That is a fine sword for a vagrant like you to bear. Stole it, I imagine."

Otchigen faced the man who accosted him. As he had thought, it was Rogdai. He had not recognized Otchigen either.

Forcing his wood-stiff back muscles to straighten, Otchigen unsheathed his sword and raised it over his head in the ceremonial challenge. In a voice cracked with the dust of the road, he said, "Who would challenge the Voyevoda of Vasyllia? Let him name the time and place for a public airing of his grievances before the Dar himself and the Dumar assembled."

Rogdai blanched and stood rooted to the spot, his mouth open.

I must look even worse than I imagine.

"I... forgive me, my lord Otchigen. I did not... Lord, I am told to watch for your arrival. The Dar awaits your convenience."

"When were you given this command, Vohin Rogdai?" Otchigen's heart lurched forward in sudden terror. Was it Lebía? Had something happened to her? Was Karakul still alive?

"Just this morning, my lord." He looked quizzically at Otchigen. "Of course," he said, more to himself than to Otchigen. "You couldn't have known. Voran has successfully passed the Ordeal of Silence. The first warrior to do so in one hundred and sixty-seven years."

To Otchigen's rising guilt, his first thought was not of Voran at all. It was worry about Karakul. But he stifled the question. No good for Rogdai to know that he seemed to care more for a Karilan foundling than his own son.

Without another word, he hurried by the fastest roads to the third reach and home. The Dar would have to wait.

⚜

OTCHIGEN EXAMINED VORAN'S FACE, not sure what he expected. It was still roughly oval in shape, his hair still the dark, almost black, color that his own had been in youth, though straiter and less unruly. The first semblance of a mustache hung on either edge of his upper lip, and a puff of dark fuzz hung on by his chin for dear life. His eyes were different, though not by much. They seemed slightly haunted. But that could have been the news of his mother as much as any supernatural wisdom attained during the Ordeal of Silence. He still looked no older than his sixteen years.

Otchigen kept waiting for some emotion at the thought of

his own son completing an ordeal that no warrior had managed to overcome in a century. He should be proud. He should be embracing him right now. Not standing stiffly before the dining table, his hand lightly resting on the back of one of the chairs. Voran, for his part, seemed not to expect much more from his father. Otchigen didn't know what was worse—the reality of his unfeeling or Voran's expectation of it.

Instead, Otchigen's heart beat with fear for Karakul. Was he well? Was he even alive? Why would no one tell him?

"I am... proud of you, my son," said Otchigen. It sounded even more forced than it did in his mind a split second before.

"Yes," said Voran, his eyes somewhere else, in some unfathomable deep that Otchigen would never reach. "Well, it's not as difficult as all that. Or perhaps it just suits my temperament."

"That it certainly does," said Otchigen. He couldn't prevent a note of derision in the laugh that followed his words. "I mean, certainly a hot-head like Mirnían was never cut out for it."

"I wonder that he even tried, to be honest," said Voran in that remarkably assured way that so many took for conceit when it was simply a lack of self-awareness. "Still, he has nothing to be ashamed of. He lasted longer than most."

"Yet he is to be Dar. I think it might rankle a bit more than you think."

"I don't see why it should," said Voran, with a tone that intended no more continuation of the present subject.

"How is Lebía?" asked Otchigen.

Voran's eyes flared for a moment. There was real anger there. Otchigen almost rejoiced to see it.

"As well as can be expected. She is only eight, you know. And she has been without any family member for the past *week*." So much suppressed blame in his voice! Otchigen wished he would let it all out in a torrent of anger. It would do both of them good.

"I found no word of your mother," he said, trying to change subject. "I did have a very..." he wanted to say terrifying, but settled for "interesting ... encounter with Semyon the Pillar-dweller. You've always been one for the stories, yes? Well, you might be disappointed to hear that none of tales about him are even close to the..."

"My lord," said Voran, his voice like a white-hot metal poker. "I believe you are tired from your journey. The Dar is expecting both of us to appear before the afternoon bell. I will have the servants prepare a quick meal for you, you need not worry. Perhaps the steam room as well? Yes, of course. You need not worry about Lebía. She is with the Dar's family for the day. Rest, my lord."

"Voran, one more thing. Semyon suggested something would happen to Karakul..." He felt too embarrassed to continue.

"Oh, you had not heard! The day after you left, Karakul was attacked in an alley in the second reach. Four men, hired by Nevida's family. He killed three of them. He is a little shaken, with a few bruises and slashes. But he is well."

Otchigen's relief must have been evident, because Voran pursed his mouth and turned stiffly away. A wave of jealousy seemed to pour off him.

"My son..."

"Rest, my lord. We leave in two hours."

❧

THE SETTING SUN painted the Chamber of Counsel with shifting shades of red, orange, blue, and purple, making the flames on the Covenant Tree dance as though Otchigen and Voran were facing the actual tree, not a fresco. This time, the Dar sat in his own throne of marble. He was robed in a deep red mantle fringed with gold that caught the light from the colored glass and sparkled. The effect almost distracted from his sudden aging, but not nearly enough.

Look at the pair of us, thought Otchigen. *Both of us are half what we were only last week, but dressed in more finery than we'd ever put on if we had any say in it.*

Voran was serious, even stately, in his cohort robe of black cinched with a forest-green belt. It was adorned with a brass buckle wrought into the shape of a falcon in flight. Mirnían, who stood across from Voran, was in the pure white of his princely office. He studiously ignored Voran. Voran didn't seem to notice, still lost in his thoughts.

The bulk of the official proceedings was over. Voran had been honored by the Dar with a drink from the Dar's own toasting horn. Voran had accepted it with a look at the Dar that had more warmth in it than Otchigen had ever felt come in his direction. He tried not to feel hurt at it.

"My dear friends," said the Dar. "I must soon call the Dumar for deliberation. They will call for an open declaration of war against Karila. The mood has been restive for a while now, and, for good or ill, Vohin Karakul's victory over the third reach's boy darling has not helped."

What he did not say, and what Otchigen had heard from Voran on the way to the palace, was that Segynduk had had to go into hiding after two attempts on his life. He and Karakul were at the moment packing their things for the journey to Karila.

"I would have kept Karakul here for as long as possible, but his victory provides us with an unexpected advantage. He has sworn his oath of loyalty to our person this morning. I do not doubt him. Otchigen, do you have any reason to doubt his word?"

"I do not, Highness," said Otchigen, trying to keep his tone neutral.

"It is as I hoped," said the Dar, sighing. "He will lead a small detachment of warriors who will go ostensibly as protection for a special embassy of Vasylli from all reaches. Segynduk will go with them. He has promised me that he will do everything in his power to defuse the fear at the rusting of the blade. With the blessing of Otar Kalun, I am providing Karila with a cutting from the Great Tree itself. Segynduk will carry it himself in a lantern specially crafted to withstand heat. It is my hope that the flame on the cutting will remain, even after removed from the city."

"That is a great gift, Highness," said Voran. "What of the rusted blade? Surely it should be removed from Karila?"

"Karakul is charged with bringing it back. Ostensibly so that our Otars can see if there are any measures that can be taken to restore it."

Otchigen winced at the Dar's apparently unthinking admission in his use of the word "ostensibly."

"You cannot entrust such a task to a new Vohin, Highness," said Otchigen. "He may not yet have the necessary... well..."

"Shall we call it authority?" offered the Dar helpfully. Otchigen nodded, feeling his cheeks get warmer as he felt Voran's gaze intent on him.

"I should go with Karakul. It will be good for him, and the Karila will surely see this as a fitting expression of our continued unity."

"Yes, I agree," said the Dar. "It will do you good as well."

Voran shifted in his otherwise perfectly straight stance.

"Does Voran disagree with the decision of the Dar?" It was the first time Mirnían had spoken. His voice was replete with scorn. Voran seemed genuinely taken aback by it. Poor Voran. He had much to learn about the world still.

"Highness," Voran did not look at Mirnían. "I understand why so little has been said of my mother's disappearance. It is inexplicable and strange, and even Semyon the stylite had little to helpful to say, as I am told. But in spite of that, surely you can see that my sister needs her father at this time? My time will be split between the study rooms and the pentagon as I enter the final years of my studies. Surely my father would not want me to flag in my warrior training?" He did not look at Otchigen, though the rising pink in his cheek betrayed much.

"Voran, my dear boy," said the Dar. "Your concern is commendable. We will get to the bottom of your mother's disappearance, I promise it. But surely you can see how comfortable

Lebía is with my daughter Sabíana and the rest of the women? She must stay here for the foreseeable future."

"This morning, she seemed content with Sabíana," Voran admitted ruefully. He shook his head, stubbornly unconvinced. "Of course, it must be as your Highness wishes. You have always been like a father to this family."

Only then did he look at Otchigen for a moment, before turning away. On the surface, it was only a straight glance. But the pleading there was strong, containing what Otchigen suspected was many months' worth of thoughts and contemplation in the silence of the ordeal. For the first time, Otchigen realized that enforced silence could have driven a lesser man mad.

He was almost surprised to realize that he was proud of his son. Perhaps something would come of him, after all.

CHAPTER 8
THE EMBASSY TO KARILA

They made a strange company—twenty mounted warriors, led by Otchigen and Karakul, a young diplomat and his wife with ancestral ties to Karila, seated in a merchant's cart laden with wares, the merchant himself guiding the two packhorses, and Segynduk on a spirited pony so small it could have been specially made for children. His legs hung almost to the ground, comically. But one look was enough to show how much the old Karilan valued the little beast. The merchant, Otchigen was pleased to note, surprised every stereotype of the second reach by being both skinny and morose. A motley company, but certainly not a boring one.

Otchigen found the days passing quickly, even pleasantly, in his conversations with Karakul and the young couple, both of whom were well-educated, with a subtle wit. More than that, Otchigen was warmed by the easy intimacy of their personal conversations, even when he couldn't hear them. Clearly, they were not long married, or if they were, then their bond was a rare one. Not that different from the bond shared by him and Aglaia not so long ago.

He tried not to think of Aglaia, though her image never faded from his heart.

About two weeks into their journey, when they were already in the heart of Nebesta, the jagged mountains of Vasyllia started giving way to the gentler, more feminine landscape of the Nebesti ranges. Crags still jutted out from the rare carn, but mostly the hills rolled like the waves following a longboat's wake. That day, Karakul had been quieter than usual, more thoughtful. The young diplomat had tried to engage him in conversation several times, but Karakul hadn't even seemed to hear. Otchigen knew him well enough to wait for him to begin speaking when he wanted.

It came unexpectedly, when Otchigen himself was lost in memories of the storytelling at his hearth when Voran was still a wide-eyed, impressionable boy of four years old, and Lebía wasn't even a thought in her mother's mind.

"My Lord Otchigen," said Karakul almost diffidently, as though he didn't want to break into Otchigen's reverie. "You haven't said anything about your meeting with the stylite. I would be honored if you shared some of his wisdom with me."

"Wisdom?" Otchigen scoffed. "Yes, I suppose there was some of that. But if I told you the pattern of his speech, word for word, you would think I was making a bad joke." The memory of the old pillar-dweller cooled him unpleasantly, but even stronger was the impression of the scene of his death. *Which had not happened and never will if I can help it.*

"There was one thing he said to me that remained with me, Karakul. If most of what he said would make little sense to anyone but me, this, I think, you will understand. He suggested to me that the capacity to love, turned inward, coupled with a powerful anger, turned outward, are a force for destruction." He would not say that Semyon suggested that those particular failings in Otchigen could break the world apart.

Karakul seemed to guess something of the like in any case.

"It's an interesting thought. What does the Wisdom of the Warrior say? 'A love so hot that it can melt the blade of your opponent'? But that love is not a love turned inward. It is a love

61

for family and city-state. I suppose that the same force of love, when centered completely on the self, could be a terrible thing. But a force for self-destruction alone, I would have thought."

"I agree. But coupled with a powerful anger? Why would that make it an externally destructive force?"

Karakul smiled, then shook his head. He said nothing, though his glance was knowing.

Of course. "I apologize, Karakul. Certainly that is exactly the kind of thing that caused Nevida's failure in the pentagon. But I still think it a sign of weakness, not a force for destruction."

"And yet," Karakul seemed unwilling to continue, pushing the words as though against an internal obstruction. "It can be destructive in the darkness of lies and treachery. For they nearly had my head on a platter, my Lord."

Otchigen said nothing, confused into silence. Was he capable of such actions? Or did Semyon mean something different? And would the reverse—a love turned outward, an anger turned inward—then be his saving grace? But how? Was not his anger turned inward making him a pitiable fool already? One who abandoned his loved ones for a fruitless search in the wild?

He could not fathom it.

🙖🙔

HE KEPT THINKING about it until they made camp under a stand of old oaks, huddling near one of the mountain springs that crisscrossed the entire landscape of lower Nebesta. As he had during this entire journey, Otchigen eschewed putting up pavilions. He had had enough of his pampered life.

Lying under the stars, too numerous to even contemplate in the nearly moonless sky, he did not hear the hoofbeats until they were nearly on top of his small company. When he snapped into awareness and sat up to see, torches already defaced the tranquil darkness. At least twenty torches, and the shifting smoke between each evenly-spaced flame roiled, hiding the exact number of riders, but giving the hazy impression of a large force.

"Karakul!" Otchigen snapped in his commander voice. "Get the men up. Horsemen approaching from the South."

Karakul was up, his sword buckled and his helm strapped on in less than a minute. The rest of the warriors took longer.

"No time to ready horses." Otchigen swore into the fog that streamed from his mouth into the chilly night air. "Well, brothers. Time to put your training to the test."

By that time, the rest of the party had awoken in the ruckus. Otchigen arranged his men in a semicircle around the cart and the civilians, enough of a space away to at least try to control the angle of attack. Though if there were as many horsemen as he suspected, that would be nearly impossible.

"Try to keep yourselves between the horsemen and our civilians," Otchigen barked. He looked around to see intent concentration on the faces of each man. No fear. No shuddering moves. Nothing but contained ferocity, waiting to be unleashed. Only Karakul shifted from foot to foot, though there was no laxness in his body. He was storing energy to be expelled like an arrow from a bowstring.

Before he could finish that thought, the torchlight expanded, so that the distances between each fire increased. They were going to try to outflank them. Damn. That's exactly what he would have done.

"Circle the cart! Go!" Otchigen commanded, and every man obeyed as one.

The moment they took their new stance, a sound ripped the air around them. As the small hairs stood up all over this body, Otchigen realized, horrified, that those were human cries. They were wilder, more unfettered than any wolf's howl.

One moment, the torches looked a hundred yards away. Then, suddenly, they were only a stone's throw in front of them. Otchigen had just enough thought left to realize that these attackers had shuttered their torches partially to make it look like they were much farther away. A brilliant tactic. There was a cunning mind behind these attackers.

Arrows fell like a summer hailstorm, and the torches retreated a few steps. In a blink, five of his men were on the ground, killed by arrows in their eyes. Not a single arrow had missed.

"Heights! What is this?" Otchigen growled, his palm sweating as he gripped his longsword.

Five more arrows flashed in the light of the torches . Five more men fell dead, arrows in their eyes. In half a minute, Otchigen had lost half his fighting force.

"Karakul, don't wait, attack!"

Otchigen and Karakul ran at the retreating horsemen, who had now turned back. Arrows sped past Otchigen's head, not striking, but close enough for him to feel the wind sliced in half. A quick half-glance to ensure Karakul was still alive, and he hurled himself at the nearest horseman. He slashed with his longsword, but the horseman's curved saber parried it easily and his horse rode past him. Otchigen, almost in desperation, grabbed the rider's kaftan and pulled him down to the ground. The man fell awkwardly, but rose up again as though the ground was bouncy. He was short, but even through his mail, Otchigen recognized a frame of wiry muscle, like a young stallion. He lunged again.

The flurry of blows was quick, but the saber was no match for the longsword. Otchigen impaled him and pushed his limp body off, clearing his blade. He had just enough time to turn around when something struck him on the back of the head, something heavy and blunt. He was on his knees, his vision dimming, before he knew what was happening. Through the dimming haze, he slashed at two horses circling him and hamstrung them. They screamed, and the mounted warriors jumped off their backs, landing on their feet like cats.

Otchigen couldn't believe his eyes. He had never seen such agility, such prowess before.

Something hit him again, and the darkness swallowed him up.

❦

THE WORLD SWIRLED around Otchigen wildly. He saw faces leering at him as strange rat-a-tat voices chattered in a half-bestial tongue. He saw the bodies of his warriors being laid down on the ground in tidy rows completely stripped of both armor and clothing. That brought him back into full realization. The throbbing racked his body, beginning in his head, ending in his feet. He tried moving his hands. They were unbound. He was unbound. So was Karakul next to him. That was strange.

The rest of the company, except for Segynduk, was dead, he saw after a quick glance around him. Even the young woman. She was also laid out, stripped, and not even next to her husband. Several of the attackers had eyes for nothing but her naked form, even though she was clearly dead.

He tried to focus his splitting vision on the attackers. There was something of the Karilans in them—similarly angled features and rounded faces, but in more exaggerated fashion. And their skin was darker than the Karilan paleness.

Segynduk was on his knees, holding the jar with the cutting of the Covenant Tree. For a moment, Otchigen was relieved to see that a feeble flame still played on the leaves. Then he realized how foolish he was.

Segynduk was speaking with the attackers in what seemed to be their own tongue, his tone still sharp with disapproval. One of the larger ones, dressed in a brown kaftan of similar make to Segynduk's own—the only difference being the wildly-colored sash of what looked like silk, which exactly matched a silk bandanna wrapped around a black fur-rimmed cap—listened to the old Karilan with amusement.

Something moved with blinding quickness in the corner of Otchigen's eye. Karakul, in full battle readiness, had run up to the vessel with the cutting and grabbed it from Segynduk. In a quick movement more reminiscent of a leopard than a man, he threw it against a stone monolith that sat in the earth like a rotten tooth of a giant. The vessel shattered and the fire flared for a moment before going out.

"You'll wish you hadn't done that," said a voice behind Otchigen. All the warriors and Segynduk had eyes only for the speaker now. Fear came in waves at Otchigen from behind. He tried to will himself to stay in place.

He turned around slowly, as though a giant hand had taken the crown of his head and was spinning him like a child's toy.

What he saw made him gag. It looked human. Or at least, it may have been human at some point in the past. There was little on that former man except yellow-brown skin stretched like a tanner's leather over jutting bones. The face had no more nose or ears, and the eyes were more red than white, bulging, as though they might fall out of the socket at any moment. The figure lay on a litter placed on the ground, swaddled like a child in furs.

"Karakul, isn't it? I've had my eye on you for a while. Yes, you'll make a fine vessel."

Karakul seemed rooted to the ground, though none of him was tied in place. He had a vacant expression in his eyes, and they kept rolling back into his head as though he were about to fall asleep or pass out.

"You're young and strong. You should manage the process of transfiguration well enough." The lips hardly moved on that skeletal face. It seemed as though the voice sounded inside everyone's head, not coming from the dried-up lips. In fact, the face had no lips to speak of any more. Just withered bits of flesh.

"It is only fair you should know in advance. I am the Raven. You Karilans may know me as the Great Changer. To be chosen as my vessel is the greatest honor offered to those who inhabit the Lows of earth."

Otchigen's eyes went dark for a moment. Then, vision. The

same intensity as when he stood before Semyon. Karakul standing on the palace turret of Vasyllia. All the people of the city assembled before him in a crowd as thick as an anthill. Karakul raised his arm, and it had a faint outline extending from it just beyond his vision, as of a monstrous raven's wing. Grey-helmed soldiers ran into the Vasylli crowd and began tearing infant children from the hands of their mothers...

"No!" Otchigen snapped back to awareness. His chest was filled with fire, but a different kind. A sureness that he had only one deed to accomplish in his life. A desperate hope that it would be enough.

He lunged at one of the attackers who stood near Karakul, grabbing the knife at his belt so quickly, the man barely had time to twitch.

"Stop him!" bellowed the Raven's voice in everyone's head.

"Karakul," said Otchigen as he plunged the knife into Karakul's heart. "I love you. You are my son."

CHAPTER 9

POSSESSION

At the command of the half-dead man, the soldiers did unspeakable defilement to the corpses. Otchigen watched it all, willing himself to remember it all. He didn't know how, but he would make these warriors pay for what they did.

Suddenly, there was not one heart in his chest. There were thousands.

He retched and lost consciousness.

You may think you are your own man. You are not. Your anger is futile. Nothing can save you. You are not you any longer. And soon, you and I will be so intertwined that there will no longer be a you or I. Far better, I think, than the intimacy of the marriage bed.

Not one flesh. One will. One mind. One desire.

To devour.

Otchigen stood in the stylite's valley. The pillar had toppled.

The body of the stylite was splayed out on one of the fallen stones. Thick metal pegs were driven into his hands and feet. His chest was slashed open.

Otchigen stood over the fallen stylite, holding the knife high as it dripped blood, dark in the fading light of an autumn sunset.

"I used to think that you would do it willingly, for hatred of me," said Semyon.

Otchigen's sense of self returned, and he felt only one heart in his chest. He screamed as he fell on his knees, clutching the knife as though he could never let it go.

"Fool!" hissed a voice to Otchigen's left. A towering figure, at least eight feet tall, dark grey like slate. It *was* made of slate, or so it looked. A man's chest on a man's pair of legs with a man's set of arms coming from the shoulders. But it had a feathered head with the crest erect, a man's eyes bulging from above a raven's beak, curved like a pair of sabres joined at the tips. Two jagged wings extended out from behind the bestial creature. It clicked its beak.

"He is mine. I have already eaten most of his will. The rest I keep for myself, so that he will know what he does in Vasyllia. So he can see the blood of his children spill in the streets."

"You have no power here, Raven," whispered Semyon, his eyes losing focus. "He would indeed have been yours forever. And your victory would have been complete. But for one reason alone."

Otchigen tore his eyes away from the monster on his left, thirsty for Semyon's words like a man traveling the desert for a week.

"Do you think you have enough power yet, Raven, to kill me? In my own valley? You are still formless. Only fools believe that the illusion of that monster-form is real."

At that word, the monstrous giant-raven shimmered as though he were a reflection in a pool.

"No, Raven. You may yet topple worlds, subvert nations to

your cause. But you shall not take my life. I, however, give it. Willingly. Not to you. To that poor wretch."

He raised his head feebly, the muscles on his neck seemingly barely holding it up.

"Otchigen. There is just enough left of you in there. Remember what I told you. And use it. You may hold off the utter darkness yet."

Then, the thought, so, so feeble.

Can a love turned outward, an anger turned inward be my saving grace?

"Yes, it can," answered Semyon in a barely audible whisper. "That creature inside you has only one use for you. To kill Voran."

"Why?" Otchigen wheezed, barely able to get the words out. "Voran is no great warrior. Why should it want his death?" He felt, with every breath, his own will collapsing as the will of the Raven clawed its way back into his heart.

"Voran is the key. It is not by accident that he fulfilled the Ordeal of Silence. He has a part to play, a very important part, in this great story."

"He is nothing more than a rusted blade," growled the bird-creature at Otchigen's left, becoming taller and more substantial by the second. "As is this pitiful vessel."

Otchigen gasped as he felt himself slipping out of his own control.

❦

OTCHIGEN HOBBLED on the road before Vasyllia in a crowd of ragged beggars. He was one of them. It was the feast day of Holy Poverty. The one day that every beggar in the outlying villages of Vasyllia would be given entrance into the first reach of Vasyllia, where each of them would receive a single coin from the hand of the Dar himself.

Voran would be there with the Dar.

He was supposed to kill Voran. He wanted to kill Voran.

☙❦❧

THE DAR SEEMED to float through a sea of ragged forms in the first reach. He was only a stone's throw away from the shuddering form that had once been called... what was it? Otch... something...

The Dar and his retinue were only two beggars away. A knife appeared in the beggar's hand. He no longer wondered at such inexplicable things.

Two young people walked behind the Dar, their eyes filled with pity. The young woman, a dark-haired beauty with piercing brown eyes, extended her hand to touch every finger that lifted toward her black velvet gown. The young man next to her had the eyes of a much older man. They were wet with tears. He threw coins to every person on whom his eyes rested.

He was...

His name was...

Voran.

The man he had to kill. He had to kill him. If he did, he would finally be at peace. His heart would be his again.

The beggar's eye fell on the young woman again. He knew her. Sabíana. The Dar's daughter.

She and Voran held hands. The ring of betrothal sparked on her finger.

They were promised to each other.

Kill him!!!

The thought was inside him, but it was not him. He hated that voice. He hated that thing inside him. He unleashed the full force of his hatred against himself for having that thing inside him.

It screamed. He felt as though every drop of blood in his body has suddenly boiled.

The dagger fell clattering to the rocks. No one noticed.

The beggar remembered himself. He remembered Voran. His son. Tears filled his eyes and he quietly wept.

Voran. I bless you. I bless you as your father. I, Otch... Otchigen. I love you more than you will ever know. Care for your sister. Find your mother. I failed you all.

The thing inside him roared with fury, and Otchigen, the former Voyevoda of Vasyllia, doubled over in pain.

❧

HE WAS in a pile of garbage outside a public house. It stank. He stank.

It was the deepest part of night, but even a moonless night couldn't hide the towering figure of the Raven before him.

"You think you've won?" It growled. "I will find another way to kill Voran. And now that you defied me, I will not obscure your mind from the horrors your body will perpetrate. You will see everything. Every death. Every treachery. Every drop of innocent blood. That is my gift to you. It is what you deserve."

❧

THE BEGGAR with no name awoke to a world transformed. Outside his hovel of sticks, assembled on the wind side of a garbage pile on the second reach, the trees were encased in ice. Branches, like freshly-minted blades, beat against each other in a military salute. The beggar stood up, every inch of his body searing in pain. The hundreds of hearts in his chest thrummed, threatening to burst him from within.

The sun breached the distant lines of the Vasylli ranges, and the ice-encased branches glowed from within. A song rose inside him with a vast crescendo, then faded again. It stopped his breath short like a punch to the chest.

"Ammil," he said aloud, remembering something.

Where had he heard that word before?

The sun's morning sparkle through hoarfrost, said a young woman's voice, as distinctly as if she were standing next to him. There was something familiar about that voice.

It was the voice of Lebía. His daughter. He was... Otchigen.

Otchigen, his heart full of the memory of the song that he did not understand, fell on his knees before the sun and begged.

"Most High," he whispered. "I am not a praying man. I am not worthy of anything you can give me. I do not ask for my will. I do not ask for my body. Only take my mind. Leave the rest for the Raven."

He heard the voice of Lebía again.

That's how the Old Tales call it. Ammil. The blessing of the Most High, you know.

He knew...

It was the last thought of Otchigen, former Voyevoda of Vasyllia.

EXCLUSIVE CONTENT: A LAMENTATION OF SYRIN

Have you ever wondered how an author goes through his thinking and writing process? Well, I've decided to share an early version of my first novel. It has elements that eventually ended up both in *The Song of the Sirin* and *A Rusted Blade*. Hopefully you'll find this glimpse into an author's process interesting. (And maybe a little hilarious. This was definitely written before I had any idea about how to craft a story).

Here, for your reading pleasure, is *A Lamentation of Syrin*: an early draft of Nicholas Kotar's *Raven Son* series.

S ome songs, once heard, are never forgotten. Songs whispered by trees to the wind, songs bellowed by one mountain peak to another, songs chanted by the Syrin, calling men to deeds worthy of legend. Young Voran, eldest son of an ancient warrior clan of Vasyllia, believed that such songs were still sung, though no one in his cohort at the warrior seminary took him seriously. Voran insisted he could hear intimations of a Syrin-song in the rustle of an alder, the cry of an eagle, the thunder of the mountain city's twin waterfalls, but the others only laughed. Especially the Dar's son Mirnían.

"Old tales," Mirnían said. It was late Leafturn, a day or two before the season of ordeal. The cohort had just left the training grounds, and most of the sweat-soaked scholar-warriors were now milling about in the open-air courtyard of the school. "You are a dreamer, Voran, not a warrior." The cohort, enamored as always of the prince with the flowing golden locks, rushed to surround Voran, eager for an unsanctioned brawl.

Voran would have none of it, not anymore. It was time to take matters into his own hands.

"You insult me, Dar's son." Voran's hand gripped his hunting knife until his fingers cramped. He had never yet openly challenged Mirnían.

Mirnían's smile was like a slime-mold hiding just under the skin of a ripe pear. It was enough to stamp out the vestiges of Voran's fear. His left hand jerked spasmodically as he attempted to loosen his hunting knife from his belt. It slipped out and clanged on the old stones, loud enough to make the other cohorts turn and look. Voran berated himself silently for reducing the impressive gesture to a parody.

Mirnían's smile faded into white fury. "You dare challenge me?"

"I do," said Voran. "Will you crawl back to Dar Antomír, or will you answer me in kind?"

Even before Voran had finished speaking, Mirnían's knife clanged point-first on the flagstones. Its sparkling pearl handle was almost obscenely clean. A mountain toppled from Voran's shoulders. He had been so sure Mirnían would simply mock him and walk away.

"Name your weapon, then, Voran." Mirnían regained his composure, though his calm was furious with potential energy. Any moment his soft grey eyes threatened to flash lightning.

That was victory enough. Voran savored it, looking away from Mirnían, calculating the number of seconds to drive him just short of mad. It was enough time to notice how thick the ice had encased the mostly leafless trees in last night's storm. The branches, like fresh-minted blades, clanged against each other in an almost military salute. Voran took it as a good omen.

"Weapon?" Voran forced his voice to remain detached. "How unimaginative, my Prince. No, I challenge you to the ordeal of silence."

Everyone around Voran was struck dumb. Even the trees hung in uneasy suspension between wind-gusts.

How appropriate, thought Voran, enjoying the faces gaping at him, that silence should greet such a challenge.

"Fool," said Mirnían, but his voice was uneasy. "You know we are still four years from our allotted time."

"Exactly," said Voran, offering no further explanation. Mirnían stared at him in amused confusion, until realization dawned on him.

"You cannot be serious," he guffawed. "You actually believe the old story?"

Voran smiled in a way he hoped was knowing and calm, though every emotion he had, and some he never imagined could exist, raged within him at the same time.

"Can you believe the absurdity of him?" Mirnían turned to the cohort, raising his voice, eager to include them in Voran's shame. Voran had a vivid image all of Vasyllia turning to look up at the eyrie-like military academy on the third reach. "Voran thinks that if he fulfills the ordeal before his time, he will be gifted by a song from a Syrin."

A few of them--the younger ones, mostly--did their best to guffaw on cue. But too many of them were silent, unsure of the outcome. Mirnían, not content with the half-hearted response, squared his shoulders at Voran like a bull preparing to charge.

"You must be completely insa..."

"Coward," Voran whispered, cutting Mirnían down into total silence. Mirnían flushed livid.

"Very well. I accept." Mirnían came forward and clutched Voran's forearm, digging the nails as deep as he could without showing the effort in his face. He folded Voran into the traditional embrace, but instead of a kiss, he whispered poison into Voran's ear: "This will cost you more than you bargained for. You think to court my sister when the time comes? Think again, half-wit."

It took all of Voran's self-control not to dash Mirnían against the flagstones.

To Voran's shock, the cohort elders agreed to sanction the challenge. Mirnían hid his chagrin in indifference, but by now reality had reduced Voran's bravado to fear. What had he done? Forty days of enforced seclusion in a locked chapel of Adonais, with only a small window to the outside world. Bread and water but twice a day. No messengers allowed in or out. Isolation from the world. Intimacy with an enemy.

Voran remained in the courtyard after all had gone home. Beneath him, half-hidden in evening fog, Vasyllia's many terraces, sculpted gardens, meandering footpaths ceased their scrambling day-life in preparation for evening. From this height, the few people still outdoors were hardly more than paint-smudges on a fresco. As human life stilled, all of nature awoke. Blade-branches continued their salute, departing swans filigreed the sky, winds howled and hissed derisively. In the lull between gusts, Voran heard the shadow of the Syrin's song again, teasing him.

He rushed home to pack his things, his heart warm again.

When he finished, he had gathered little more than a few old shirts, faded wool breeches, and his sword. There was little else in his room to take. His grandfather's old mail-shirt and peaked helmet was black with disuse and silvered with cobwebs, but he would hardly need those. He caught a glimpse of an ugly carving, probably done with a child's hand, hanging on the wall. He hadn't seen it before. It was a Syrin, but her head was far too big for her eagle body, and her feathers looked vaguely scaled. Of course, Voran thought with a smile. Little Lebía's parting gift. If anything could sustain him during the long days ahead, the thought of his little sister would.

"After all," he said aloud to the ugly creature, "you are the real reason I'm mad enough to do this." He put the carving into his bag.

"Voran, can I come in?"

Mother's voice had that pining quality it always had before a long journey or absence from home. Voran sighed at her intrusion, hoping that she did not hear. He turned around. Her cheeks were flushed red. She had heard.

"I know you want to sleep," she whispered, tiptoeing with her voice. "But this is the last chance I'll have to speak to you for a very long time, I fear."

"What troubles you, Mother?"

Aglaia's headscarf was crooked, tied up with shaking hands-- not the servants', so much was clear-- and she had forgotten several of her temple rings. A few greasy strands of greying hair peeked out like mischievous children. All this was highly unusual for the leading lady of the Vasylli military court. Voran took her hand and sat with her on his windowsill.

His gable-window revealed a new Vasyllia. The lanterns hanging on every two-story house of the third reach set alight the dancing spume of Vasyllia's famed twin waterfalls. It looked as though the stars had descended from the spheres for a single night of revelry. Something deep within the city summoned Voran, and not for the first time. Not the Vasyllia built of wood on the face of the mountain. No, that was little more than a mask. The real city lying in the rocky bones of the mountain--chambers and caves groping inward and downward--<u>that</u> Vasyllia whispered to him, though he could not parse out the words.

"It's your father," she said, wrenching Voran from his contemplation.

"Mother." He no longer tried to hide his annoyance. "Is this the time to discuss Father's--"

"Hear me out, my falcon." She pressed Voran's hand and bit her lip, but the tears were already glistening. "He's fading, Voran."

"Fading? Mama, do not you think you may be exaggerating a little?"

She shaded her eyes with her free hand, leaned her face into her palm, and began to sob. She had never before cried in his presence. In spite of himself, Voran felt his skin curdle against his shirt.

"I'm sorry, Mother," he whispered. "I didn't mean..."

"No, no, my falcon. It's not your fault." She wiped her nose and tried to smile. "You're so busy with your training. You don't have time to notice. Lebía is still too small to understand. But a wife knows. Something in his spirit has broken. It's as if he no longer cares about his Dar, his city, his people. You know how full of life he was. Now, he is a shadow of himself."

All this was the last thing Voran wanted to hear. He had managed to steel himself for an ordeal no youth his age had attempted in generations. And now, he had to deal with his mother's fantasies? It was too much to bear.

"What does Dar Antomír have to say about this?" he asked, hoping to find an easy way of redirecting her worries.

"He noticed it as well. That is why he is sending him as emissary to Karila."

With a sinking feeling, Voran realized what she would ask, and every muscle in his body rebelled.

"I worry, Voran," she retorted quickly, raising her hand before he could interrupt her. "I have a presentiment that something will happen in Karila. The rumors are more than dispiriting, you know. Not just the usual Karila threats to break off from the Three Lands. Surely you've heard of the nomad armies beyond the Steppelands."

"Silly rumors, Mother."

"I want you to go with him."

He wanted to scream at her.

"Mother, I will not forego the ordeal of silence because of a rumor."

"Voran, why must you do this? If you ask me, it seems you resent Mirnían for not preferring your friendship as he used to before. This is little more than a rooster's strutting."

She was partially right, of course. Voran looked away from her, back down to the enchanted vision of the hidden Vasyllia. It calmed him again.

"Mother, can you believe me if I tell you that for me, this ordeal is more than a contest between me and the Dar's son?"

"I don't believe you." The tears welled up again.

"I do not lie to comfort you, Mama." Voran caressed her hand with his thumb. "It's about the Syrin-song."

Her eyes opened wide and she stiffened. Voran could sense her anger rippling outward.

"What?" she whispered, as though she had lost her ability to speak. "Do you imagine you will soul-bond with a Syrin? Voran, don't be a child! I'm asking you to take a man's place by your father, and you insist on playing a game merely to coddle your wounded pride."

"It's more than that." How could he make her understand? "Sometimes I wonder if Adonais, the Syrin, the Heights...if they are even real..."

"A sore on your tongue, Voran!"

Mother never allowed herself to curse anyone, much less her only son. Voran's anger warmed to match hers.

"Do you wonder at Father's fading, then? A life of the sword, a life of unswerving servitude to those who are stupider, cruder,

less noble than we. A life of constant deprivation, wet, cold,
hunger, death at an early age. This is the life of a warrior. Of
course Otchigen fades. He has lost faith in Adonais. If I cannot
find mine, will I not fade too?"

"Oh, Voran," she touched my cheek, all motherly concern
again. "I did not know of your doubt."

Voran hardly knew himself, before he uttered it aloud. But
the words, once spoken, engraved their truth on his heart.

❦

VORAN SLEPT BADLY, bothered by vivid dreams. Otchigen
featured in all of them, the worst was a nightmare where he
sprouted raven wings and grew a beak for a nose. Although
absurd in the remembrance, it was horrifying in the experience.
As soon as he awoke, Voran slipped, bare-footed and undressed,
into the hearth-room. There lay Otchigen—familiar thick white
braid and tightly curling black beard surrounding a perfectly
human nose—in the sleeping embrace of three hunter-borzoi.
When he saw Voran, Otchigen rose and smiled, brightening the
entire room with his usual impish grin. What could Mother have
meant? This was Father at his best.

The breaking of their fast was somber. Mother was tear-
stained; Father was disturbed by her unease. Lebía still slept, and
Voran did not want to wake her. They spoke of banalities over
their cold pork—still unsalted, Voran thought with pleasure. It
was as though Voran was not about to undergo an ordeal that, in
all reality, was fodder for legends.

Then the sky broke upon their heads. Lebía shrieked from
the upper story, ripped out of child-sleep. Mother went a few
shades paler, if that was possible. Only Father smiled, and it was
like a cup of wine for breakfast. He nudged Voran gently toward
the door with a quick, intimate inclination of the head. Voran
smiled back.

All it took was a touch, and the door slammed open. For a

moment, in confusion, Voran thought the sky was a grey mirror shattering. With none of the sweet patter of hail, slabs of ice shattered on stone like glass. The trees writhed like things possessed of unquiet spirit-life, hurling the ice at each other as though they were children in the middle of a very serious snow-war.

"It's only the thaw, silly boy, with a little bit of wind." Otchigen laughed, enfolding Voran in a single massive arm.

"I know that," Voran said, his pride stung, which only increased the flood of Otchigen's laughter.

The air was rich with a kind of loam-smell that only teased the nostrils one or two mornings in late autumn. The smell of the very earth taking a deep breath before the long sleep.

"A good omen, that," Otchigen nodded at the cataclysm unfolding before them.

"For you or for me?"

"Both, my boy. Have you never heard it said that rain is good for the day of your wedding, but ask for ice-storms on the day of your death?"

"Father?" Voran's insides had frozen over with the landscape to hear him speak flippantly about such things.

"You go to your death, Voran, make no mistake. When you come out of the ordeal, you will be a man of second birth. Your boyhood will be left behind, nothing more than skin sloughed off."

It heartened Voran to hear him finally say something about the ordeal. He pondered Otchigen's choice of words. They were pregnant with meaning that eluded Voran's grasp.

"In what way do you go to your death, then, Father?" Voran asked.

Otchigen considered his answer for a long time. Or so Voran thought. When he looked up at Otchigen--still so much taller and stronger than I!--he seemed to have wandered somewhere else in his thoughts.

"Father?"

He snapped as if awoken from sleep. Now his smile was frosted, almost mask-like. It chilled Voran even more deeply than the ice breaking like glass on Vasyllia's mountain-bones. Otchigen didn't answer Voran, turning back to the hearth where Lebía slept again, wrapped in an old quilt on Mother's lap. How quickly child-sleep had reasserted itself. Voran wondered when again would he ever sleep so fully and carelessly.

☨

"I DON'T EXPECT I'll be able to finish the ordeal, Voran." Mirnían spoke loudly enough for the entire cohort to hear. All of them eagerly accompanied the ordealists to the very doors of the chapel. "If you think you will, you are mistaken." Words innocuous enough in themselves, but laced with a threat no more obvious than a secret blade worn in the boot. Voran was sure Mirnían had managed to smuggle one past the elders.

Voran scrounged for an answer, but their arrival at the doors precluded any retort—witty or otherwise. All chatter ceased, cut off with a barely audible intake of breath from every member of the cohort. The chapel was rarely used by the scholar-warriors, and even when used, the doors were always open to the entry. Closed, they fulfilled an obvious purpose—not merely to prevent entry, but to discourage even the thought of it. Every hand-length of carved stone burst out in vivid reliefs. Images of beasts clawing their way out of the granite, half-breeds like wolf-men, leonyns, bull-headed giants. At first, Voran thought they were intended by the artist as a threat to the viewer, but above them, at the juncture of the two doors, towered the summit of Vasyllia with three sunbursts—the symbol of Adonais. The beasts were fleeing the power of the Heights, Voran realized. The implication of the artists was clear: those who enter are of the beasts, and lest they die to their own selves, they will not withstand the bright power of Adonais.

Father was right. This is an ordeal to the death.

The doors opened inward at a thrust from the eldest in our cohort. Beyond was nothing but unadorned stone. Stone walls, stone floor, stone rib vaulting, a single granite altar at the end of the rectangular nave. With a thrill of pleasure, Voran realized this chapel had been carved directly out of Vasyllia's mountain wall. There was no place closer to the summit than this. No wonder the ordeal was hardly ever accomplished, even at the allotted time. The very air hummed with the grace of Adonais.

As the doors closed on us, just before the ordeal officially began, Mirnían seized Voran's gaze and smiled with no warmth in his eyes.

"Beware of sleep," he said.

Thus the torture began.

Voran awoke in a cold sweat to see Mirnían towering about him, eyes wolf-lit.

Voran glimpsed the glint of steel flash in Mirnían's grasp, but it disappeared as soon as Voran tried to find it.

Voran fell violently into forgetfulness.

Voran fell even more violently into uneasy wakefulness.

The days stopped connecting to each other.

Voran awoke, head pounding from uneasy dreams, hair soaked with sweat. Mirnían was nowhere to be seen. A messy heap lay next to the altar. It could not possibly be Mirnían. Voran approached quietly, checked by the sound of sobbing. Mirnían lay on the ground, knees tucked under his chin, moaning. He looked hardly human. Perfect curls were matted and stank. Straight white teeth stood out like a sacrilege in a face filmed over with dirt. Voran reached out to comfort him, but the eyes that met his gesture flashed feral, then subsided again into pain and weeping.

The nightmares grew worse after that.

The more Mirnían descended into his own inexplicable darkness, the more Voran tried to extricate himself from him. He deepened his senses to catch the elusive Syrin-chant, but he was quickly disillusioned. He remained on his knees before the altar of Adonais, head bowed and hands outspread, for hours at a time. All he got for his pains was sore knees and two hot coals in his back where Mirnían stared at him with shadowed eyes. He repeated the words of high prayers, but his mind wandered after the first three words. He stared out the window, focusing on the details of the subtly changing landscape. Other than a vague unease in the pit of his stomach at some unusual discoloration in the highest leaves of the Great Tree, he felt no special illumination. Even Lebía's carving inspired nothing. The strongest emotion he felt was desire for sleep tugging at his eyelids.

The snows came, leaving a pregnant calm blanketing Vasyllia's sleep of an early morning. Voran awoke before the light. Mirnían slept, as he did most days, hovering between bouts of angry pacing and attacks of the same darkness that left him sobbing on the hard stone slabs.

The door nearly burst off its hinges, so loud was the knock. Mirnían flew up, his hand over his heart, chest heaving. Voran merely froze in place. Nothing but a calamity could induce anyone to break the silence of their ordeal. Lebía, he thought with dread.

"Open the door, Voran, or they'll break it down!" The moment he spit out the words, Mirnían realized he had lost the challenge, even if only a niggler would hold him accountable under the circumstances. Voran ran across the stone floor, his echoes rushing to get ahead of him. Please don't let it be Lebía, he thought.

Voran threw open the doors, expecting he knew not what, but certainly not little Lebía herself, face whiter than the new-fallen snow, save for two greyish lines down the sides of her mouth where the tears were still etching deep into the skin. Dar Antomír himself stood by her, a thick wooden staff in his hand. Voran, in confusion, fell down on his knees before both of them.

"Father?" Mirnían's voice was thick with disuse. "What is the meaning of this? How can you allow anyone to break the seal, much less your own august self?"

Dar Antomír never looked at his son. He had eyes only for Voran and Lebía.

"My poor boy," he said, and Voran saw that he had the same tear-engravings on his face that Lebía did. "Your parents, Voran. They're gone."

L ebía was finally in bed. The house was overrun with the Dar's specially selected servants and chaperones. Two tall guards in full armor stood at the door of the house, each holding a fluttering banner--a golden Syrin in full flight on a black field--the sigil of Dar Antomír and the Clan of Cassían. Having given his steward a final instruction regarding tomorrow's continued fallout from Aglaia's sudden disappearance, Voran sought the haven of his rooms.

He had not had a single moment to stop moving, much less process anything that had happened. Now he wished for nothing more than the pleasant lie of sleep.

Sleep avoided him as though he were plagued. Thoughts tussled in his mind, each insisting on his full attention. A heavy knot sat in his chest and refused to be budged. Voran lay with eyes open to the darkness until the room seemed to spin around him. He sat up, but that did nothing to dispel his restlessness. Finally, he stood up. Putting on his boots and wrapping himself in an old, faded travel cloak, he climbed out the window and slid down the carved wooden columns to the gardens below. The guards did not even notice him.

He breathed with relief, but the knot in his chest did not dissipate. The thoughts began to crowd their way forward again. Thrusting them back with as much strength as he could muster, he nearly ran from the house.

Later, he said to his thoughts. Leave me be for a few moments.

It rained all that day, until not a spot of snow was left on the ground, though all that remained of the passing storm was tattered rag-clouds. By now, it was well past dark, and even the house-lanterns were mostly extinguished. Voran found himself walking a neglected dirt path, near one of the two waterfall-fed canals. The first-reachers believed it dated to the reign of the first king, Lassar of Blessed Memory. It led to an old stair carved into the mountain, its entrance hidden by ivy. The eroded stair climbed all the way to a ledge where two giant stone chalices collected the twin waterfalls for Vasyllia's canals.

As Voran looked up, wondering whether he should attempt the climb at night, he heard a whisper on the wind. Gooseflesh washed over his hands, up his arms, and down his back, and for a moment all thoughts stilled. A wave of pleasure washed followed, so that he almost fell back. Smiling, he began to climb.

The first few cracked steps were so large he had to climb upward with his hands. At the halfway point, clambering like a spider up the precipice, he looked back at nighttime Vasyllia. Below him was darkness, except for the Temple plain at the far end of the city, sparkling with lanterns like an inverted night sky. Even though it was dark, the piebald bark of the Great Tree glimmered faintly, as though it alone could reflect starlight. The gabled houses to either side of the two canals directly below him looked like toys, thrown about randomly by a giant-child.

He had the curious sensation that he was that child, and Vasyllia was his for the taking. But Lebía's tear-engraved face intruded on his thoughts, and the sudden surge of inarticulate emotions shook him so fiercely that he almost fell.

He leaned forward until the world stopped spinning.

Not yet, he told his emotions. You will have free rein soon enough.

As though in answer to his thought, the shadow of the Syrin-song sounded louder than ever. He closed his eyes, savoring. It sounded as if the mountain itself, the trees, the clouds whispered only for him. He hardly noticed that he once again climbed, twice as quickly, and the ledge was already within sight in the half-moon's light, though smudged by the misting falls.

The song infused him with a few drops of needed strength, and he silently gave thanks. A hot dagger of grief pressed its point at his chest, but he found he could keep it from plunging through to the heart, if only for a few moments more.

Just as he reached for the ledge, Voran's right hand slipped, and the abyss yawned beneath him, eager to swallow him whole.

He clung with his fingernails to the ancient rock, trying his best not to move, not even to breathe too loudly. A sudden wind, so fierce that it seemed in league with the abyss, whipped at his cloak as though he were a longboat hurled down-river. Just as quickly, the wind retreated, leaving behind nothing but the hiss of dry leaves from the city below.

Voran hoisted himself onto the ledge, wet from the exertion and the mist, his heart beating louder than the thunder of the falls. He leaned back against one of the stone chalices--each taller than the Great Tree, and probably just as old--and closed his eyes. His back hummed with the pounding of the waterfall.

When he opened his eyes again, the tableau before him seemed to swallow him up, and he thought he would never be able breathe again for the beauty of it. At his feet, a carved stone dragon's head spit the gathered falls at the city. Something cracked in his chest. It felt as though his heart was filled with rot, and all of it gushed out in a moment together with the waters flowing down the mountain to the sleeping city. Voran's breath began to choke him, and he was forced to let go. The tears flowed out, and he began to sob, his body heaving like a child's.

So much had gone wrong. Mother had been right about Father. He had faded, whatever that meant, and it must--it must!--have something to do with his disappearance and the massacre of the Karilan embassy. But he could not understand what happened to his mother. She would not simply leave Lebía. It was too ridiculous to contemplate. But Voran had never loved as his parents did. He did not know what sort of madness love was capable of inspiring.

Lebía's face kept reappearing in his mind, each remembrance a fresh plunge of the fiery dagger. He forced himself to think about her without letting the panic overwhelm him. He was responsible for her now. He must provide for her. He was all she had left in the world; she was all he had as well.

His pain for her obscured his ability to think clearly. He

could see no easy path ahead of him. His heart was urging him to follow Otchigen's tracks, to search the wilds for Aglaia. But surely that was madness. He was only sixteen years old, hardly tested, not prepared yet by his incomplete military training. The Dar would not allow him to leave the city, now that he had no proper guardian.

Lebía would have to be taken care of. The house would have to be overseen, the orchards and gardens guided by the hand of a master. He would still have to finish his studies. How would he be able to do all?

Then there was the continuing problem of his conflict with Mirnían. Would the prince take the opportunity, now that Otchigen's house tottered, to dispose of Voran permanently?

A single ray peaked out over the mountains and alighted on Voran's face. A perfect wedge of geese passed overhead and the sun followed them, as though tied to them by gossamer threads. Rising up from the earth, an aroma of fruity mustiness suffused Voran, until he felt half-drunk with it. Birches after a night's rain. Silence.

Voran was freed from thought by the sight, though an ember of pain still smoldered in his chest. He knew now that it would never go away, but there was a quiet acceptance, even pleasure, in that thought. The morning was truly wiser than the evening, as the Old Tales would have it. He set aside all looming decisions, and stood up to brave the descent back into the city.

As he approached Otchigen's house, the dappled light revealed not only the Dar's square banners lazily ignoring the wind, but four smaller triangular ones eagerly trying to run away from the poles holding them back. Two had the black swan on silver water, two were merely black.

Voran's heart leaped at seeing the first—Sabíana's sigil. He did not know whether that leap meant joy or fear. He suspected it was more the latter, though not without some of the former. The black banner was the military academy's standard. This was highly unusual, to have representatives of the Dar's house and the academy come to one's home.

Upon entering, Voran stopped to consider an impossible sight—Lebía, wrapped in an old felt coverlet, sat on Sabíana's lap by the hearth. The purple under her eyes was gone, replaced by the creases of a smile. Her fingers busied about some sort of colored string, and she did not even raise her head at Voran's entrance. Sabíana looked at him, her eyes still, and nodded gently, not wishing to distract Lebía.

Voran had not seen Sabíana in several months, but even so short a time had transformed her. Swan-curved bust, olive skin with cheeks ruddied by the wind, brown hair no longer a mess obscuring her face, but a latticework of carefully arranged braids and curls. Only sixteen, and already a woman. But the warmth spreading through him at her beauty was nothing to the joy, poignant as a needle-prick, of seeing the two of them in such calm contentment. He still had a family, he realized.

On the other side of the hearth-room stood Elder Pahomy himself in the ceremonial black robes of a cohort father flowing about his abundant figure. Voran motioned him silently to the stairs leading to Otchigen's study.

"You do realize no one believes Otchigen is dead except the Dar," said dour and jowly Elder Pahomy, after they had dispensed with the usual pleasantries.

"What do you mean?" asked Voran, surprised by how quickly he got the point.

"Surely you have not been so housebound, Voran?" He shook his head, jowls following chin.

"It has only been a day, Elder. A day worth never remembering." Voran closed his eyes and stretched, relishing the pop of his shoulders. "Forgive me, I did not sleep this night."

"Yes, I understand." There was unexpected softness in the old warrior's voice. "And I am sorry. But you must hear what is being said. It is important that you consider well what to do next, for your sake, but even more for the honor of your sister."

"Honor? What do you mean?"

He sighed, calling to mind a smith's bellows. "Rumors fly faster than a kestrel in Vasyllia. Already many say that Otchigen lives, but he has fled into the Steppes. Some go so far as to call your father a traitor to Vasyllia. Worse, some are suggesting that the massacre of the Karilan embassy was his doing."

At first, Voran did not even understand what the elder said. It was too ridiculous.

"My father has been Voyevoda of the city, the drudge of his beloved Dar's every breathed and unbreathed wish, for over twenty years. This is how he is repaid?"

"I do not say I agree with them." Elder Pahomy leaned both hands on the parchment-strewn table between them. He lowered his voice with a wary look at the door. "But consider what reason people have for speaking so. Otchigen's grandmother was Karila, you see the proof of it in your own black hair, so rare in this sea of fair-haired Vasylli. Every other member of the embassy was brutally murdered by unknown enemies. Of your father, no sign. Nothing."

"And so some consider that proof enough that he arranged the massacre? For what possible purpose?"

"Oh, do not be thick, my boy. Piece it together."

Voran knew it without being told. Rumors of nomad armies, Karila growing restless of its subservient position in the Three Lands, Vasyllia becoming fat and complacent in the relative peace of the last few centuries. It would provide an imaginative mind with fodder for quite a tale.

"What do they say about my mother? Do they think she is traitor as well?"

"No," whispered Elder Pahomy. "She is old Vasylli stock. Thank her for the blessing of your green eyes. You would perhaps be as reviled as your father is right now, had you inherited his Karila-black eyes. Those who speculate on her fate suggest that she went mad and fled Vasyllia."

"It makes no sense. Why would my mother, a woman many

considered the guiding light of court life, suddenly run away the moment she heard an unsubstantiated rumor about her husband's death? Or treachery...It is not in her nature. She has always been strong. Even stronger than my father, in some ways."

Voran's voice faded. He considered the mother that had wept in his room. That picture did not match his memory of her. Something had happened to her.

"Voran, my boy." Elder Pahomy came around the table and laid a meaty hand on Voran's shoulder. Its weight was comforting in its sturdy reality. "I agree with you. I have known Aglaia since before she came to love the wild youth that was your father. I have seen the flowering of their love. I know the strength of the bonds uniting her to you and little Lebía. She would not have willingly left you. There is some foul play here. Do not doubt it."

Anger flared inside Voran. "Mirnían? Is this the doing of the prince, his way of punishing my insolence?"

Elder Pahomy sighed and turned away, crossing his arms over his chest, though it was so large he could hardly get them to link. He looked at Voran intently, as though his gaze could milk his thoughts like a cow's udder.

"You wrong Mirnían and you do yourself a gross injustice by even thinking such things! Are you truly such a child, Voran?"

Voran flushed in embarrassment, his stomach dropping to his heels.

"Forgive me, Elder. I hardly know what to think, much less what to say or do."

"Listen to me. You are not alone in your misfortune. The Dar himself sent me here to tell you that if you wish, you may continue your studies at home. I will personally arrange for your cohort elders to come to this house regularly to oversee you. Occasional training bouts with your cohort members, nothing too strenuous at first. I believe you can complete the academy in two years."

Three years early. No one had ever managed that before. It was an appealing challenge, especially after Voran's recent failure.

"The Dar is to provide for your household out of his personal gold," Elder Pahomy continued. "Lebía is to be finished together with Sabíana. You understand what he intends, I think."

It was practically an offer of marriage. Vera's heart did a somersault, tried to break through his ribcage, then subsided in annoyance.

"But." Elder Pahomy's voice changed. There was a hint of anger, no more than the humming of a taut bowstring. "I will tell you something that the Dar does not wish you to know. Do you understand me? I brave the Dar's displeasure by revealing this to you, boy. Try to live up to my trust."

Voran stood up straighter. He suddenly became very aware of his hands. They seemed large, ungainly, uncomfortable in any position he held them.

"Of course the Dar will send his best warriors to staunch the wound of the failed Karilan commission. He will never allow you to go with them, so do not even consider it."

Voran's face sagged with disappointment.

"However, I will offer you this, Voran. There is always need for replenishment in the ranks of the Warriors of the Word. As it happens, there is a detachment patrolling the wilds near the Karilan border. They are some of the most dour and unpleasant fellows you will ever meet, but if you want to search for your father using more...unconventional means, I will speak to the Dar on your behalf."

The Warriors of the Word. Even in the most ancient of the Old Tales, they were a telling presence—an almost fanatically secretive warrior cohort as disciplined and austere in their mind as in their body. It was said that—outside of necessity—they only ever spoke one word. What that word was, or why they chose such a strange discipline, gave rise to the most fanciful of speculation. Voran had not believed they existed outside of stories.

The sun broke through and streamed into the room in rays as distinct as Adonais's three sunbursts. Voran turned to the study's window overlooking Otchigen's extensive orchards. The snow was falling again, slowly obscuring the trees. Their private river was languid, viscous like syrup. It would freeze over very soon. Hardly the time for a journey to the far reaches of the Nebestan border with Karila, especially with all the disquieting rumors. He could be going directly into the maw of the same shadowy beast that had devoured his parents.

What the Dar offered Voran was far more preferable. The more Voran considered it, the greater he acknowledged the honor of it. By all rights, this should be the moment when Otchigen's house should fall. The Heights know there are enough vultures in the third reach who would gladly take Aglaia's orchards and Otchigen's place at the right hand of the Dar. Instead, Dar Antomír intended to raise their fortunes higher than any other family, even going so far as to stop a mere step shy of declaring his intention to join with them in matrimonial union. Most importantly, Lebía would be taken care of, effectively the Dar's ward. When things calmed down a bit, Voran would have enough influence at court to effect whatever means he wished to find his parents. It was truly a gift worthy of the brightest Dar of Vasyllia's recent memory.

"No," said Voran. "I cannot accept the Dar's offer."

Despite the promptings of his reason, his honor, even his common sense, Voran loathed the prospect of rolling about in his own fat. He would never rest easy while his father's name remained besmirched. He would never be calm while there was even a chance of his mother wandering the wilds in search of her beloved husband. No, he would take the mad path, whatever dangers lay on the road, and whatever hardships awaited among the Warriors of the Word.

"Speak to the Dar for me, Elder. He may not understand why I choose to go to the far frontiers to join the Warriors of the Name. I would not have it thought that I am not grateful to him for his boundless generosity. All I ask is that you intercede, in your own name as well as the name of Otchigen's disgraced house, that Lebía be cared for in my absence."

TWO MORNINGS LATER, Voran awoke to warmth and sun, as though the day itself was a dream of summers past. The sparkle on the river was so inviting that Voran hurried to wash himself in the frigid water. Not bothering to dress fully, he ran out, barefoot and in a single linen tunic, to hurl himself into the water before his mind had a chance to convince him of his madness.

It was like dying and coming back to life again. Or so he imagined, as he sat on the bank, trying to master his body's shaking.

Dar Antomír had been more than accommodating. He had named Lebía Ward of the Dar and had outfitted Otchigen's house with a full complement of servants, chaperones, and mentors, some of whom he was beginning to resent for taking such swift control over the household. It was all done so deftly that Voran found himself with nothing to do except pack provisions and clean his grandfather's mail, helmet, and sword. Somehow, he also had to come to terms with leaving Lebía behind effectively as an orphan, all the while itching on the inside to be on his way. It nearly tore Voran in two.

For Lebía, he said to himself. I must find them for Lebía's sake, if not for my own.

"Voran? Is that you?" The voice froze Voran in place. Absently, he found it amusing how swimming in a half-frozen river had less of a glacial effect than that voice at this particular moment.

"Sabíana, forgive me. I am not decent." He couldn't decide whether to stand or to remain seated for propriety's sake, and the resulting movement twisted his body into a half-reclining position that nearly tumbled him back into the water. Sabíana laughed.

Two days ago, after Elder Pahomy and he had finished speaking, Voran was eager to see Sabíana. When he returned to the hearth-room, however, Lebía was curled up on one of the borzois, asleep, and Sabíana was nowhere to be seen. Voran had been surprised at the dull ache in his stomach, but he dared not seek her out.

Now she came of her own volition, and at the worst time possible.

"Come, Voran. I'll wait for you in the house." Her manner was just as familiar as before, in their long childhood friendship. It was strangely discordant to see a vision of beauty speaking to him with such casual intimacy.

Somehow Voran managed to make himself presentable. When he entered the hearth-room, Sabíana sat by the fire, her eyes brilliant with tears. Lebía's arms were draped around her neck as she reclined against her.

"Voran!" Lebía jumped up and latched herself to his own neck. He twirled her as she loved so much. Her laughter was like butter on sunburnt skin.

"Sabíana says I can come live with her for a time. Is not that wonderful?"

She would be safe. Thank Adonais, she would be safe.

"Voran," said Sabíana. "You must not fear for Lebía's sake. I will take care of her in your absence. Promise me you will not worry on her account. You will have enough cares out in the wilds."

She looked at Voran straight in the eyes, completely unaware that something had changed between them. He found it impossible to return her gaze, but the moment his eye chanced on some other part of her, it fled in fear from her hand to her shoulder to her bust to her face, then threatened to repeat the loop again. He closed his eyes, breathed deeply and tried to smile, though it felt like a grimace. When he looked up again, her eyes—how brown they were, like a plowed field after rain—were laughing at him.

"Sabíana, you are too good." He managed not to croak.

"Good. That's settled then," she said, still looking straight at him. He steeled himself and looked in her eyes. Gradually, something in her expression changed. The ruddiness in her cheeks became a flush, and she looked down. Her breathing was shallow and quick. Voran wanted to embrace her violently.

"And promise me you will come back soon," she whispered, her flush extending all the way to her ears.

"I promise," said Voran, raising a trembling hand toward hers. She flinched at the touch. It was like white-hot metal.

"I think I had better go," she said, still not meeting his gaze.

"Thank you, Sabíana. Thank you for doing this."

She looked at him, smiled wistfully, and walked out, wrapping her head and shoulders in a heavy black shawl. Voran stood in the falling snow, watching Sabíana melt into the flakes.

He was no longer going merely to find his family. He would prove himself a man to Sabíana. No matter what happened, he would not return until he could present Sabíana with a hand worthy of the golden ring.

Somewhere, deep inside, another emotion warmed him with a different fire. He imagined the anger in Mirnían's face as he told him of their plans to marry. It was glorious.

„The Dar cannot spare ten swords for your journey, Voran," said Mirnían, visiting Otchigen's house unexpectedly the day before Voran's journey. "Recent scouting reports from Nebesta suggest we may have been remiss in ignoring the rumors about nomad marauders. The Dar is reassigning eight of them to increase the number of scouts patrolling the Nebestan wilds."

Liar, thought Voran. You could find no other way to pay me back for your failure in the ordeal. But he bit his tongue. Mirnían--emotionless but for an ironic half-smile--sat back in the carved high-chair Voran had offered him.

Dar Antomír had assigned Voran and nine older warriors to protect a convoy of supplies--new parchment for mapmaking, rope, furs, axes, knives, and other necessities--for the outpost of the Warriors of the Word. Even four was a meager number, considering the unsettled state of the Three Cities after the Karilan massacre, as well as the daily threat of predators.

Having only two swords was an invitation for disaster.

Mirnían yawned, left arm hanging limp from the chair-arm.

To his own surprise, Voran was bitten by nostalgia at that gesture. Something about that particular pose of the overtired prince. Grudgingly, Voran wished he was capable of doing the noble thing and approach Mirnían with an offer of truce, if only for the sake of childhood friendship. Now it would seem a cowardly attempt to curry favor.

"I am sure you and Dubían will manage," said Mirnían, barely stifling another yawn. "In any case, what should worry you more than anything is early winter storms, and two additional swords will be little help turning back a whiteout."

He rose and turned toward the door without another word or even a glance of farewell. Nostalgia died, replaced by bitterness.

"You needn't have come yourself, Mirnían." You should have stayed in bed where you belong. "Sending a boy would have been enough. It would have more suited your manner, in any case."

Voran expected an explosion of anger. Instead, Mirnían shook his head and drooped a fraction in his shoulders.

The setting sun dipped below the apple trees in the orchard, washing over Mirnían, transforming him into a carved likeness of an ancient king. His red and gold surcoat, trimmed with fox, sparkled as though washed in gold-flecked water. Even the child-puff of his blond beard gathered years in the stark light, and the thin aureole around the grey in his eyes shone out.

"Voran, I know you regret the loss of our old friendship," he whispered, though the sound seemed to resonate. "I do as well. But some things cannot be stopped. It is better to accept them, not wish for a lost treasure that will never return."

Voran lost speech. Mirnían spoke as a future king, with charisma emanating from his mien, his white skin rosy with sun, his tone. At that moment Voran understood that men would follow Mirnían gladly to death, or worse, if only to feel the kiss of his goodwill for a moment.

Still, Voran did not understand why Mirnían had decided their friendship was reduced to a treasured memory of the past. He sensed that Mirnían indicated much between his words, something a more patient mind would understand.

"Mirnían," Voran said before Mirnían could leave the room. "What happened there, in the chapel? Why were you so shaken by the ordeal?"

Whatever calmness had been in the prince's face, it was wiped off in a moment. Mirnían bit his lower lip and his entire body stiffened. He stood there, locking eyes with Voran, frozen in indecision. He let out a sharp hiss of breath, wet with spittle. Having turned sharply to the door, he strode out, his boots thrashing the floor. Voran winced as he heard him barking at his retainers in front of the house. A plaintive yelp from a dog that misread his mood properly. A furious flurry of booted feet.

Voran felt cheated. There should be at least some sort of triumph in ruffling Mirnían's perfect composure. Instead, he ached deep in his stomach. There seemed no hope for a renewal of their friendship, and the loss bothered him more than he expected.

ॐ

THAT NIGHT VORAN lay awake interminably, distracted from sleep by his thoughts. When he did fall asleep, it was not to rest, but to a dream so vivid that he was tempted to call it a vision. He saw an endless road through a forest overgrown with tattered ivy and moss. A vale, not a living plant to be seen, filled with miles upon miles of human bones. Smoke and fire and swarming clouds of ravens over a high mountain plain strewn with the bodies of dead warriors. A river of water washing them all clean, until there was nothing but a field of grass so green it hurt the eyes, dotted here and there with perfect white blossoms that smelled of tuberose and orange. A single fallen warrior in white, his pale face and black hair so familiar, so familiar, his chest gaping red...

He woke, his heart pounding, his shirt soaked through. The fallen warrior in the dream was Voran himself.

These images niggled at his mind as the convoy of three mule-driven carts gathered in front of Vasyllia's gates later that morning. It was a motley group. Most were simple first-reachers--two stonemasons, their wives, and a little girl with a quick smile--with two weeks' worth of supplies on their backs. These were family members of those outposted with the Warriors of the Word. Several others--already seated on cushions, legs wrapped in sheep's wool--were second-reacher merchants hoping to make a final profit before winter in some of the villages along the way. Their droopy fur-rimmed hats and wide scarlet pantaloons amused Voran. He was sure they would be freezing by the end of the week, even with their leg-wrappings. How many days would it take before they dipped into furs intended for the market?

The massive bronze doors in Vasyllia's marble walls needed

all of ten door-wardens to pull open. As the doors creaked like two old women being awoken too early in the morning, Voran stared at the arch above them—a fanciful carving of two oaks leaning toward each other. It struck Voran that they were carved with more than mere skill. There was a playful kind of affection in the carver's tools, some inspiration that made the trees look as living as two entwined lovers.

Voran's thought shifted with a sharp pang to Sabíana. It pierced, but with the pain came a pleasant warmth. She had not come to see him depart, and he had been loath to seek her out himself. Now he cursed himself for a fool. He would give anything to look at her again before they left.

What about Lebía? said his conscience, rebuking. It was best for her not to see me, he retorted, though his conscience remained unconvinced. Voran hoped Lebía would understand.

Finally the doors groaned their final complaint, revealing the long plateau before Vasyllia, farmland already harvested for the long winter. Dubían rode in front—a mountain leading a pack of sheep, thought Voran—leaving the rearguard to Voran. As Voran passed the last door-warden, an older, bearded warrior named Rogdai whom Voran had met once or twice, he heard the man spit loudly.

"Traitor's spawn," growled Rogdai.

Voran's anger was swift and warm in his chest. He spun his filly about and pulled hard enough for her to rear. Rogdai looked up at him, nonplussed, taunting with his eyes. Voran wanted to reach for his sword, every muscle tensed painfully. Why not? This old goat would be an easy kill, and it would send a message to others that slander of Otchigen would not be tolerated.

You have never killed. Is this the time to begin?

For a moment, confusion filled Voran. The thought was so loud in his mind, he was sure it was spoken. Was it even his own thought? Sensing his unease, the filly snorted and tossed her head back, snapping him back to the present. He forced his breath to slow, intent on Rogdai. He found that he had lost any interest in the insult. With hardly a glance at the man, he directed the filly back to the convoy, already some distance ahead. She immediately fell into a canter.

As they joined the others, Voran looked back once more on the receding mountain city. His eye caught the top of the Great Tree. There were brown spots amid the golden winter-leaves.

Voran shivered and wrapped himself with the edges of his cloak. Yet another source of unease. The leaves of the Great Tree never fell, only turning gold during winter, then reawakening to green with the coming of spring. Not a single leaf had fallen in Vasyllia's history. What sort of omen was this?

A torrent of laughter distracted Voran. Dubían was trotting toward him, his head craned back, broken teeth catching the sun. His face was as red as his frothing beard.

"Vohin Voran," he somehow managed to fit in between the torrents, "I truly believed your temples would burst, they pulsed so violently when Rogdai insulted you! I am in awe of your self-control. Would that fool had insulted my family so, he would find no more use for his spit-shine helm."

And he exploded in laughter again. It seemed Voran would have no lack of interesting conversation along the way.

⚜

A FEW HOURS LATER, his thoughts stilled for a time by the Valley of Vasyllia sprawled before them, Voran rode a little behind the company in silence. No one sought his conversation, and Dubían was engaged in what he probably imagined was singing. For the entire first day they crossed sparsely wooded country through stands of birches and colonnades of alder. As the sun dipped below the summits, bloodying their snowy tips, the small company narrowed into single file onto a dirt path. It twisted sharply into the gloom of huddled conifers before them.

"Vohin Voran," called Dubían, appearing suddenly at Voran's side. "May I suggest you vary your aspect a bit from 'brooding horror' to something more pleasant? You are frightening our fellow travelers."

Voran smiled. "Am I? Forgive me, I was thinking of the Great Tree." Voran relapsed into silence. Dubían fell into an easy trot next to him, keeping an occasional eye on the convoy ahead.

"Ah, you saw the browning as well?" Dubían whispered. "What do you think of it?"

"I hardly know what. It chills my heart, but perhaps that is merely my mood after my parents' disappearance. All the same, the Karilan massacre, the rumors of nomads marauding far Nebesta, and now the Great Tree..."

"Tell me, Voran," Dubían's eyes, usually creased with laughter, assessed Voran critically. "Did you know that the Great Tree was called the Covenant Tree in ages past?"

"I know my Old Tales, Vohin Dubían." Voran twitched his reins, annoyed. The filly responded by reaching around and trying to bite his leg.

"Perhaps not as well as you think," Dubían said, no longer looking at Voran. He did not wait for an answer before clicking his tongue. His black mare rushed back to the front.

What could he mean? Voran was raised on the Old Tales, as was every Vasylli child. First among them, repeated most often during the storytelling on Market Day, was the tale of the covenant between Dar Lassar of Blessed Memory and the Harbinger, the Mouth of Adonais. A covenant whose visible sign was the ever-flowering Great Tree in the middle of Vasyllia. The death of the Tree, or so warned the Old Tales, meant the breaking of the covenant. Surely Dubían did not actually believe that? The covenant was nothing more than an instructive story, a teaching aid to help children of all Three Cities understand the importance of Vasyllia's primacy over the other cities.

Lost in thought, Voran hardly noticed the approach of the Nebestan border. Here the way to Karila and the outpost of the Warriors of the Word diverged from the main road, and the merchants took their one cart and turned back to Vasyllia.

The dirt track entered the thickest forest they had yet seen. The moment they entered, Voran strained to breathe. The trees stood so closely compacted that not only light, but even air seemed shut out completely. Voran gagged at the stench of something rotting, so thick he seemed to wade through it. No birdsong, no rustle of leaves, no gurgle of rushing water. Not even the sound of footfall. All was muted to an indistinct, pervasive murmur.

Cobwebs the size of a horse leaned curiously into the road, heavy with moisture. Trails of lichen waved the travelers on, thought there was not even a breath of wind.

This forest is alive, Voran thought, and shivered.

"Make camp!" called Dubían, though the sound died a hand's breadth from his lips. The convoy stopped, the first-reachers morose and tense.

Voran dismounted and tied his filly to a branch. As he approached, Dubían nodded silently in the direction of the deep forest away from the path. At first, Voran couldn't understand what he saw. They walked some distance into the thick trees, hunched over most of the time because of the low-hanging branches, many of which cracked loudly and fell as soon as they touched them. They were nearly on top of it before it took form in his mind, though he had been looking straight at it for several moments.

A deer, ripped apart. Voran's stomach curdled.

"Look, Voran. There's something very wrong here."

He was right. The deer was savaged by a beast, that was obvious. The teeth-marks were wolfish, though bigger than any wolf Voran had ever seen. But the wolf had not eaten anything. It had just ripped apart the animal and left it to die.

"No natural wolf does this," said Voran. "It is something a man would do. A madman."

"A man, or a creature of the Darkness."

The Darkness. That domain of everything the hidden recesses of Vasyllian imagination could conjure: cannibal hags living in huts on chicken-feet, giants with wolf maws for heads, many-headed flying serpents, the Raven. Voran wanted to laugh, but he felt that if he did, the trees would not take it kindly.

"Come, Dubían. We must move through this forest as quickly as possible."

"Voran, this is the Forest of Morrok. It will take us a week at best to pass through."

Silently, both warriors returned to convoy, swords bared.

Voran was driving sharpened stakes around their night-shelter when one of the women screamed. He ran toward the scream, careful not to be heard as he ran, the better to come unawares on whatever beast lay ahead. Dubían, barely visible in the corner of his eye, did the same. He was remarkably quiet for such a large man.

One of the women was on her knees, shrieking wordlessly. She gripped her hair as though her life depended on not letting go. Her fingers shook with the strain. At her feet lay the body of her husband, his throat torn out.

Spots danced before Voran's eyes, and his legs turned to water. He had to look away. Closing his eyes, he gradually felt the roiling waves turn back to earth. He forced himself to look back, and as the nausea reared up to attack, he beat it back. Forcibly controlling his breath, he crouched to take a closer look. He had never yet seen the face of violent death.

It certainly seemed a wolf's doing. The jagged rip of the flesh looked similar to a wound one of his cohort members received at the tender mercies of a half-starved hunting dog. The man's right fist was clenched. With an effort, Voran forced the fingers open, revealing rough bristles in the man's hand, typical of the thick nape of a wolf.

Strange. The hairs are black, not grey. A black wolf?

The few tracks that the beast left were wolf-shaped, but they were unthinkably large. The size of a bear's, at the very least.

He pointed Dubían to the woman. Dubían, his face red with worry and his eyes on the verge of tears, embraced her and began to mutter something quiet and soothing as he led her back to camp.

"Vohin Dubían, we'll have to set up a watch this night." Voran said, after Dubían returned. "You take the first while I bury him. I suppose you will have to bring a priest from Vasyllia in the spring to sing the service. I doubt we'll be able to do it before."

Dubían stiffened, unhappy about something, but nodded agreement.

At that moment, it struck Voran. He had not heard any shadow of the Syrin-chant since they left the main road.

৩৯৩

VORAN MANAGED to stay fully awake during his watch. But when all the travelers had risen and were beginning to prepare breakfast and break camp, the killed stonemason's wife was not among them.

"Dubían, did anyone leave camp during your watch last night?" asked Voran as the bleary-eyed bear-man emerged yawn-first from his tent.

Dubían stopped in mid-yawn and raised both eyebrows.

"No, Voran. Have you lost someone?"

Voran turned and ran into the forest, senses alert. Now that he was attentive, he could smell it. Blood.

Her dead body lay next to her husband's. The beast had killed her, dragged her out into the forest, and dug out her husband from his makeshift grave. Voran thought he had known fear before. He was wrong.

A twig snapped behind Voran. He spun on his heels, sword up. Just before him, face white with horror, was the little girl. She screamed. Behind her, running, were her father and mother, followed by Dubían. The woman stopped, both hands shaking before her mouth, but the father ran to his girl and picked her up, turning her away from the carnage.

"We are going back, Vohin Dubían," the man said. "It is but one day's journey back to the last village we passed. We must leave this accursed forest now."

Dubían's eyes shot toward Voran. He seemed hesitant to answer.

"Must?" said Voran. "We must? Sudar, you knew the dangers when we set out. These two unfortunates left the safety of camp. The beast doesn't attack openly, surely you see that. If we stay together and no one does anything stupid..." He trailed off, dismayed at the hostility in the stonemason's eyes.

"You filthy third-reach child," he spat. "What are you, sixteen years of age? Learn some humility, boy, and let your elders give orders. Why Vohin Dubían didn't rebuke you after you assigned him the first watch last night, I do not understand."

Voran was about to retort something about first-reachers knowing their place, but he saw confirmation of the man's rebuke in Dubían's abashed expression. Embarrassment rushed in and silenced him. The stonemason turned away from him in disgust.

"This whelp can do as he wishes, but we are going back to Vasyllia. Our brothers in the wild will have to wait until spring for their comforts."

"Likely as not, they will not even notice our lack," said the woman, doing her best not to look either at the corpses or Voran. All of them turned away and walked back from the camp.

Voran began to shake from rising fury. No, these weaklings would not prevent him. Nothing was going to stop him from reaching his goal. He would travel on, alone if he must. Bear-wolfs be damned!

"I am not coming with you," Voran announced to their retreating backs. Dubían spun around, his red anger matching Voran's.

"That's enough, Voran," he whispered. "Fall in. We are going back."

"You are going back," said Voran, drawing his sword. "I will go on."

"Idiot boy," muttered Dubían into his beard. "Sheath your sword, or I will carry you bound back to Vasyllia as a traitor."

The bear-likeness grew in Dubían. He seemed to swell in size, his arms alone wider than tree-trunks. He bore down on Voran, each step scattering dry leaves and twigs down the incline in mini-avalanches. His breath foamed into storm-clouds in the crisp morning air. Suddenly afraid, Voran dropped his sword and fell on one knee, covering his head with both arms.

He heard the slash of steel as Dubían picked up his fallen sword.

"You forfeit your right to use this," he growled. "What the Dar sees in you, I do not understand. Sudar stonemason, can you handle a sword?"

"Not much worse than you, bear-man," the mason said.

"In your fantasies, perhaps." Dubían laughed and threw the sword at the mason. Still holding the girl, the man reached up and caught it without any effort. Even in his shame, Voran's heart briefly flared with proud warmth. Only Vasyllia raised such commoners.

"Voran." Dubían no longer laughed. "Give me your helm."

Voran hesitated, mouth agape, but at Dubían's glare he yanked it off and extended it in a shaking hand. Dubían grabbed it and tore the horse-hair from the peak. He hurled the dishonored helm down on the forest floor. Raising one booted foot, he stamped on it as though it were no more than a toy. To Voran's shock, the helm crumpled into a misshapen lump of iron, ear-guards detached, nose-guard bent completely backward.

It was the ultimate shame for a warrior, especially a junior. It would probably mean expulsion from the military academy. Voran saw Elder Pahomy's jowls quivering in disgust, Mirnían's eyes triumphing at his defeat, Sabíana's equal in their derision.

"Come, Voran," said Dubían. His face was pink, and Voran

thought he sensed the big man's regret at reacting so hastily. "Let us not quarrel before our fellows. It is not seemly for Vasylli."

They trudged back in the direction of camp. Only after they had walked for a quarter of an hour did Voran realize something was wrong. They had not arrived back at camp, though they had walked much farther than they should have. Dubían stopped, a thin line of sweat on his brow the only sign of his distress. He faced the stonemason, who still held the girl, now asleep in his arms.

"Sudar. I regret I must tell you that we have lost our way."

S abíana despised high day afternoons. Once a week, it behooved Adonais--or at least the clerics who spoke in his name--to confine all members of the Dar's household to the palace. All anyone wanted was to be outside for as long as possible before the winter, but instead they were ordered to dedicate the half-day to the constant restoration of the Temple holies. Today, a day of deep blue winter-sky and crisp air, Sabíana's sacred work was the restoration of an ancient banner. She tried to remember how many weeks in a row she had slaved over this half-tattered rag. She lost count at seven.

It was a large square banner depicting a Sirin in flight. The style was archaic: flattened and abstract. The woman's head was badly fitted to the body by an almost nonexistent neck; the wings were far too widely outstretched, the eagle-talons looked twisted with respect to the rest of the body. The face was long gone, and even in the weeks of her work, Sabíana had managed only to finish the eyes.

To her dismay, she saw that one of the eyes was bigger than the other. How had she not noticed it before? She silently groaned.

The two other girls joined her soon after she began, sitting opposite her at the long table brought into her chamber once a week. They sat demurely, not daring to speak, though the stifled smiles warned that soon decorum would fail, and the gossip would begin. Sabíana wondered if she would even have five minutes of silence with her thoughts.

"What a fine figure that Yadovír made at Temple today, did he not?" attempted one of them, a pale girl of thirteen.

"Yado--who? Do you mean that *first-reacher*?" hissed the other, appalled.

Sabíana groaned, audibly this time. The girls' heads dropped back to their work, and she won another few minutes of blessed silence.

Now that her fingers overcame their initial clumsiness to act of their own accord, Sabíana could finally give a little rein to her thoughts. The Sirin, and the old story about the gift of her song to the brave warrior who would complete an ordeal before his time, made Sabíana think of Voran.

He was so different from the child she had known so well. Little Voran was awkward and thoughtful, round green eyes often on the verge of tears. Mirnían abused him constantly, only ceasing his rough physical play to ridicule the size of his nose or the dirty black of his hair, but Voran only loved him the more for it. Sabíana herself couldn't help but tease the quiet boy mercilessly, although she felt foolish doing it and regretted it afterward.

She came to Voran's house eager to renew their childhood friendship. After entering the military academy, Voran hardly crossed her path except during the services at the Temple, where she glimpsed him among the silent ranks of boy-warriors, but he was not allowed to speak to her there. But before her stood no child. He was more than halfway to manhood, his reticence and thoughtfulness overlaid by a throbbing, silent anger.

It was not that, however. There was something new in his eyes, a depth of feeling she only saw in people much older. After she left him and Lebía, her stomach ached dully for hours, hounded by his intense, penetrating gaze. She did not know what to make of it.

"My father told me that the traitor's son got what his father deserved!" The younger girl's face was red with annoyance. Sabíana guessed that she had stumbled into the middle of a heated argument.

"Your father is an upstart second-reacher who speaks far more than he should," said the other girl, smirking.

"Silence, both of you," Sabíana snapped, smacking her palms on the table. Both girls jumped, and the younger immediately melted into tears.

"Enough of that, Malita." Sabíana tried to make her voice soothing, but it came out raspy. She patted the younger girl's hand. The girl jerked it away. "Tell me, what traitor's son are you talking of?"

Malita flushed and shook her head, continuing to sob into her skirts.

"Go on, I won't bite you, I promise." But I may bark some more, if you don't speak quickly. "Surely you don't mean Voran?"

It was as if her face were brushed over by white paint, then quickly repainted again in dark red.

"Malita, I am ashamed of you, to be spreading rumors. Do you not realize how much Vohin Voran has lost already?"

Malita looked up, lips pursed in exasperation. "I am only repeating what everybody knows. Mirnían himself..."

"Do not presume to name the prince without his honorific."

Malita stamped her foot, and the tears flowed anew. The other girl, embarrassed to be the cause of her friend's fit, interjected, though not looking up from her embroidery.

"What Malita was trying to say, Lady Sabíana, is that it is common knowledge that Dar Antomír, after assigning nine warriors to accompany Vohin Voran into the Karilan wilds, changed his mind and sent only one warrior. Many in the city believe it to be a sign of the Dar's acknowledgment of Voyevoda Otchigen's betrayal. Many also..." The girl's voice tapered off. She had finally gathered the courage to look at Sabíana, but immediately faded back into dumbfounded fear. Sabíana realized her fury must have been visible in her face. She would have to work on her composure. Later.

Without saying anything more, Sabíana rose, pushing back the wooden bench so fiercely it turned over on the floor. Both girls, shoulders tensed and hunched over, looked very attentively at the embroidered clouds above the Syrin's head. Without giving them another thought, Sabíana pulled the door open as hard as she could. It crashed, and the young sentry at the door, a boy of no more than fifteen, jumped half a foot into the air.

"That will teach you to sleep on your post, soldier," she said as she passed him. "Let that be the last time, or Elder Pahomy will hear of it."

The boy straightened and saluted, fist to chest. Two beads of sweat streaked down his cheek.

Sabíana hid a smile as she hurried down the tapestried hallway. She really should not enjoy rattling the men so much, but the pleasure never lessened for its frequent repetition.

Her mirth quickly subsided. Mirnían. She knew it was he. Her father would never have sanctioned Voran's honor guard of nine to be reduced to one. Arrogant, pathetic weakling! He couldn't best Voran in the ordeal, but was this how low he would stoop to get his revenge? And how did he manage it without Father knowing about it?

Past the rounded archway, a wall of icy wind slapped her face before she could descend the stairs hugging the sides of her turret. Perhaps it would be best to avoid the outdoors. Reaching the new rushes strewn on the bare ground below, she turned left through a heavy oak door that creaked with disuse. A curving staircase stood beyond the door, rising to a latticed hallway lined with white stone pillars in the form of trees, with nothing but the clouded sky as a roof. At the end of the curiously open passage stood another wooden door with a carved Syrin in a tree. Her father's private room.

She raised her fist to knock, but stopped. Voices, raised. She put her ear to the door and closed her eyes. Mirnían, his tone plaintive, petulant in his most childish way. Father's answer. Angry. Gooseflesh prickled her neck. Father had not been this angry in a very long time. She screwed up her eyes, trying to make out the words. Her father was speaking.

"You dare to excuse..." Something muffled, maybe *treason?* "Can't understand. How..." again incomprehensible "without my knowing?"

Mumbled whining. "How...responsibility...if you question my every..."

Sabíana pushed gently, and the door opened just a crack.

"You have no authority to do this, my son! Do you not realize what you've done? You have involved others in an action that subverted the will of the Dar. Openly! And why? Because you are a child. Do you not understand that such seeds of future dissent can grow into dynastic war? Do you not understand that there are many who would leap at the chance to make their fortunes by advancing your Darship before I die?"

Sabíana shook her head and cursed Mirnían silently. What a mindless idiot! Was this the Dar Vasyllia deserved after someone like her father?

"Father, I acted as I believed correct. You did not hear the reports of the scouts. I did. The more men we can send to protect our border, the better."

"Nomad armies, Mirnían?" The derision in Father's voice was painful. "Nomads don't have *armies*, my boy. Organization is not their strength." He sighed heavily.

Sabíana heard more in that sigh than exhaustion. It was old age. The thought maddened her, and she pushed the door and advanced on Mirnían. Seeing her, he took three steps back and raised his hands in self-defense.

"You idiot, Mirnían! Why is it that I, a *woman*, can see the ramifications of your actions better than you can yourself? Have you stopped to think for even half a second? What if Otchigen is found to be a victim? What if everything that is coursed about in the city about Voran's family is proved false? You have allied yourself with the babblers. When Voran returns, justified, you will look weaker than the son of the Voyevoda. Is that a good vantage point for a future Dar?"

Mirnían opened his mouth, but could find nothing to say. Frustrated, he turned away from her and vented at the Dar.

"You favor him over me, Father. Don't try to deny it."

Sabíana gasped. Dar Antomír's eyes filled with such pain, she wanted to cry herself. His breathing grew raspy and irregular, and he slumped like an emptying wineskin onto the wooden chair he much preferred to the throne in his receiving chamber.

His simple black tunic and white hair were stark against the opulence of velvet blue and gold hangings decorating the walls of the circular room. Mirnían started forward, only now aware of his father's fatigue, but Sabíana motioned him to stop with a flick of her fingers. He obeyed.

Sabíana sat on her knees by her father and rested her arms and head in his lap. His thick, battle-worn fingers absently stroked her head. Slowly, she could feel his breathing still. She allowed herself the luxury of relaxing her own breath.

"Father, I'm sorry. I didn't mean..." Mirnían began, looking away from both of them in confusion.

"My children," said the Dar, his voice thick and heavy, "I don't like to admit it, but I think perhaps Wicked Woman Age may be catching me after all." He laughed ruefully.

A weak knock on the door barely made an impression on Sabíana.

"Ah, I almost forgot," wheezed Dar Antomír as he gently raised Sabíana and pushed himself back up with a wince. "Mirnían, we must go to the session of Dumar today."

"May I come today, Father?" asked Sabíana.

He looked at her with some surprise.

"I cannot bear another minute with that forsaken banner," she whispered, her eyes downcast. She hoped that her expression was suitably submissive.

Dar Antomír laughed. "Come, daughter. You've deserved it today."

Only stopping for a moment to put on the ancient silver crown wrought with white gold flowers blooming, the Dar walked out of his private chamber, leaning on the arm of Sabíana.

৩≈ঔ

THE DOUBLE DOORS of the Chamber of Deliberation opened inward. A towering fresco adorned the far wall, an ancient mural of the Great Tree. Two-tiered galleries of wood lined either side of the rectangular room, where the assembled Dumar, the forty chosen representatives of the people, all stood to greet the king. In each of the four corners of the room stood a great free-standing carved tree--a birch and an oak near the entrance, and a beech and a maple at the opposite end. They were neither painted nor gilded, the old marble smooth and glistening with age.

Sabíana needed to use every ounce of self-control not to skip ahead and shriek in excitement. Her father had never before let her take part in official business, despite three years of nearly constant nagging on her part.

Mirnían at Sabíana's right was smirking. Sabíana realized that her mouth was open. She shut it, so suddenly that it echoed.

"Fish-lips," he whispered. Heat flooded her face. She looked at her feet, trying to console herself by imagining ingenious forms of torture Mirnían would never expect.

"We are but visiting today, my children," said Dar Antomír to the serious faces of the men before him. Do not let us deter you."

A young steward of the palace, so inflated with his own importance that Sabíana was afraid he might pop like a bubble of scum on the lake-surface, shouted at the top of his voice, "Dumar may be seated, with the blessing of the Dar. Chosen speakers of Dumar, step forward for counsel."

Assembled Dumar sat, the room echoing with the swish of overcoats and the thud of sheathed swords against wooden benches.

Mirnían led Dar Antomír to a raised platform next to the oak statue, where the Dar mounted a simple throne of white marble, raised three steps above the platform floor. Mirnían then took his place at his right, a step lower in a smaller seat of malachite. Sabíana sat on the Dar's left on a throne of pink granite. It was very cold, and soon her back side was an ice block.

Two bearded warriors, helmed and bearing spears, walked

onto the empty floor between the galleries. Between them stood a third man, round and red-faced, his thick black beard striated with two bands of white. He wore a brown long-coat stamped with repeating red roundels. The robes peeking out from under his heavy coat were as long as the coat itself, reaching almost to his feet, which were shod in bright red shoes with toes slightly upturned. Compared to the Vasylli men, who favored knee-length tunics and breeches, he dressed like a woman. Sabíana could not decide whether he was worth pitying or laughing at.

"Don't offend our guest, Sabíana," whispered her Father. He was always adept at reading her mood. Either that, or she needed to redouble her work on her composure. "That is the dress of Nebestan nobility, my swan. You may be surprised, but Lord Farlaav is one of the more moderate dressers."

Sabíana stifled a guffaw, but not very well. The Dar smiled in the corner of his eyes. She could sense Mirnían bristle at being excluded from their shared joke.

Lord Farlaav bowed to each warrior in turn, and they turned back.

"Assembled Dumar! I am Lord Farlaav, Steward of the Voyevoda of Nebesta. Many of you know me well."

A smattering of grins and laughs burbled in one of the galleries. Sabíana wondered what sort of shared history the Steward of Nebesta could have with the commons of Vasyllia.

"Don't believe his serious demeanor, my swan. He is known as the most ferocious drinker in the three cities."

Sabíana was shocked. The Dar chuckled.

"Never believe the surface of things, my dear. One does not find rocks flecked with gold on the bare ground, but only in mines. Look deeper." He resumed gazing at the Dumar. Sabíana resolved to do her best to begin mining the personalities before her.

"I need hardly tell you, my brothers, that this Leafturn has been uncharacteristically severe. It is not enough that we Nebestans must endure the flatulence of your Vasylli mountains bearing down on us all winter, but now you send ice-rain on our heads for good measure!" He waved dismissively at the other gallery, drawing jeers and hisses, all of them in jest.

"Time you fat Nebestans shared some of our winter hardship, Farlaav," said an old courtier with two massive mustaches that covered his mouth so completely, it seemed his mustaches were speaking for him. The entire Dumar broke out in laughter. Farlaav bowed to the speaker, then gestured at him rudely. Sabíana gasped, offended. Mirnían laughed.

"That is nothing, sister. There will be much more of that. Can you stomach it?" His manner was even more offensive than the gesture. Sabíana ignored him.

"As always, fair Buyan," said Farlaav, "you do great honor to your city with your oratory. But I beg Dumar to hearken. All jesting aside, Nebesta is in need of aid."

Sabíana was surprised at the sudden strain in the room, tense as a mountain cat just before the pounce. She stiffened without thinking. Looking at her father, she was surprised to see that his expression was pained. There was much she did not understand, much spoken silently between the lines.

"Nebesta harvests later than Vasyllia, as you must know. The ice-rain has destroyed most of our crops. If Vasyllia does not aid us, many will starve this winter."

The silence was more deafening than the chorus of laughter.

"Father, why is no one speaking?" whispered Sabíana. "Surely we must help Nebesta."

Dar Antomír looked at her a long time, then smiled weakly. He shook his head once and pointed back at the Dumar. Pay attention, his gesture said.

Farlaav turned around, looking at each person of the forty in the face, finally looking up at the covered platform. His eyes met hers, and she looked away, unable to bear their intensity. There was piercing fear and pain in those eyes. Surely the Dar would sanction the requested aid.

Finally, one of the second-reachers stood up, his pantaloons more than usually wide. A pheasant feather stuck up from his beaver hat, quivering with every word.

"Lord Farlaav, we of the second reach will be very pleased to offer your city first access to next Market Day. We will be selling last year's surplus at a very low price.

Sabíana was appalled. Lord Farlaav fears for the life of his entire people, and all we can offer is to sell him salted meat, stale bread, and sprouted cabbage? Our own poor don't eat that food.

Sabíana looked at her father, her right palm outstretched--why are you not doing something?--her head craned forward. He did not meet her eyes.

"Wait," he whispered. "I have to believe there is at least one man brave enough to do what is necessary before I shame them all like children."

Lord Farlaav waited. With each passing second, his shoulders slumped lower, as though the burden he refused to show in his face were finally beyond his power to uphold.

"Thank you, Vasyllia, for generously aiding your sister cities," Lord Farlaav said. "Ever you have been an example and a bulwark for those under your primacy."

He looked directly at the Dar for the first time, the intensity in his gaze like metal fired to a white heat. The Dar parried his gaze, biding his time. Sighing, he began to get up.

"Shame!" echoed a voice from the galleries. "Shame on Vasyllia! Have we forgotten our calling?" A young man, richly attired in a pale purple-dyed wool cloak with a clasp on his shoulder that blinded with its polish, strode past his fellow-Dumar into the center of the room, facing Farlaav. Sabíana had never seen him before.

"Are we not a High People, chosen by Adonais? Does not the pledge of his covenant stand in the center of this glorious city? And does not the covenant state that our sacred duty is to provide for our sister cities in all hardship? Shame on your coin-hoarding, you second-reaching graspers! Shame on your manicured orchards and flower gardens, first-reachers! Have none of you seen the browning on top of the Great Tree?"

The assembly seethed with flailing arms and shaking heads and stomping feet.

"Who allowed you to speak, milk-sucker?"

"Someone teach him manners!"

"This is what comes of allowing young men into Dumar!"

The Dar's mouth was cracked open in surprise as he sat back down, intent on the young orator. He shook his head and raised his eyebrows, admiring.

"Sit down, Sudar Yadovír," said Kalun, the willowy chief cleric of Adonais in a watery voice. "You embarrass yourself."

Is _that_ the Yadovír the girls were tittering over? Sabíana certainly saw nothing attractive in his oily hair and effeminate gestures. There was something snake-like about him.

"Father Kalun, is that you speaking?" continued Yadovír, almost screaming. "Is this the keeper of the _Sayings_, the interpreter of the Old Tales? Are you the mouth of Adonais? Fie on your faithlessness!"

Two of the military men in the front row jumped up, intent on charging the young man, physically held back by their peers. Several hats had already been thrown down to the speaking floor in disgust. Yadovír walked on them, coldly assessing the mass of indignant faces. A roar went up at this act of dishonor. The raised platform began to shake under Sabíana's feet.

"The covenant is a story, you fool!"

"Who allowed him in here?"

"Your head will make a fine decoration on the city walls, boy!"

Kalun stood and raised his hands, his face even darker than his long, thin hair and sparse beard. The mass stilled, but the tension hummed on the air still.

"Sudar Yadovír. We are all very impressed with your faith. We are all touched with the sincerity of your beliefs. But let grown men do the work of state building. The covenant, though undoubtedly true, is more of a spiritual reality than a physically binding contract. We do what we can to help our sister cities, as long as our own Vasyllia is not left the poorer. As for the browning of the tree..." He smiled like a father at a silly child. "As Lord Farlaav said, this Leafturn has been uncharacteristically severe. Even the Great Tree suffers from it."

Yadovír was unimpressed. He turned and addressed the Dar directly, immediately raising the ire of assembled Dumar.

"Highness! I beg you to hear Lord Farlaav, and to grant his wish. Surely we can do better than sell surpluses!"

Mirnían was on his feet, face red with anger. "Dog, do not presume to address your Dar without being spoken to!"

Dar Antomír placed his right hand on Mirnían's arm, shaking his head. His fatigue was completely gone, to Sabíana's joy, and his voice echoed in the room.

"Assembled Dumar! The Dar's treasury will compensate the merchants for the value of your complete reserves. All the surplus food in Vasyllia must go to Nebesta. Sudar Yadovír, we would ask you to coordinate this matter with the second reach. Lord Farlaav, if you would join us for supper, we would be most grateful."

Lord Farlaav, eyes on the verge of tears, bowed low to the Dar.

"Thank you, Assembled Dumar. We will trouble your convocation no further."

Dumar sat down again and continued their daily business. Sabíana was fascinated at how quickly they all subsided. Even those sitting next to Yadovír seemed to bear him no grudge, though they were willing enough to tear him in piece just five minutes before. Her eye wandered to Yadovír. He stared at her.

Sabíana flinched and tried to look away, but she could not. Something held her eyes in place. She felt the sweat break out on her temples and the back of her neck itch furiously. He smiled and nodded, once. The effect was like drinking a purgative, and she nearly spit out bile.

There is something wrong about that man, she thought. He is dangerous.

"Well, that was unexpected," said the Dar, looking at Mirnían. "Perhaps there's hope for us yet."

Mirnían eyed him with weary annoyance. For once, Sabíana agreed with him.

"Surely you don't mean that foolish fellow, Father?" asked Mirnían. "I know of him. He is an ambitious young first-reacher. Some sort of tragedy in his past, and it drives him upward. You know the type. He will call the moon green if it suits his purposes."

The slap was so quick that Sabíana herself flinched. An angry welt grew on Mirnían's cheek, and the artless shock on his face was perhaps the first natural emotion he had shown all day.

"You weary me with your doubts, Mirnían," said the Dar, and walked past him.

Mirnían looked after him, his expression inscrutable. For the first time in a long time, Sabíana pitied her brother. Today was not his best day.

"Mirnían," she said, embracing him with her left arm. "I think you are right. There is something wrong with Yadovír. You and I will have to protect Father from him."

He shrugged her off with an expression he reserved for spiders and snakes.

"Don't you have a banner to embroider, sister?"

ALSO BY NICHOLAS KOTAR

The Song of the Sirin
The Curse of the Raven
The Heart of the World
The Forge of the Covenant

ABOUT THE AUTHOR

Nicholas Kotar is a writer of epic fantasy inspired by Russian fairy tales, a freelance translator from Russian to English, the resident conductor of the men's choir at a Russian monastery in the middle of nowhere, and a semi-professional vocalist. His one great regret in life is that he was not born in the nineteenth century in St. Petersburg, but he is doing everything he can to remedy that error.

CPSIA information can be obtained
at www.ICGtesting.com
Printed in the USA
BVHW030508150321
602455BV00001B/41

9 781732 087378